# CLAIMING CHAOS

## FIRE WITCHES OF SALEM
## BOOK THREE

# CARRIE PULKINEN

# CHAPTER I

# ASH

"Poor Patrice." My heart hammered in my chest as we crept toward her house. Chrys didn't bother with shadow spells or cloaking for whatever she'd done inside, and the icky, sticky dark magic funk bled out into the yard, making my stomach lurch.

A knee-high leaf pile stood to the right of the walk, a discarded rake lying next to it. The wind had blown through the mound, scattering half the leaves she'd gathered across the yard. One crunched beneath my foot as I stopped at the bottom of the porch steps.

Yep, I had taken point on this endeavor, which was *so* not me. But I could reveal her spells without a potion, so there I was, leading the way into who knew what madness. I still couldn't wrap my mind around Chrys being involved in this ordeal...especially not her being a murderer. She was Cinder's best friend, for Hecate's sake.

Chaos stood behind me, so close I could feel the heat radiating from his skin. Ember positioned herself behind him, with Miles and Shade taking up the rear. I cast my spell, sending magic onto the house, and golden sparkles gathered around the door and windows.

"Of course there's a ward." Ember bounded up the steps ahead of me and examined the magic. "Have you seen anything like this before?"

I joined her on the porch. "See how the energy moves in waves, rather than shimmering? She cast it with a lower vibration than a light witch would dare. It reminds me of the electrification spell BMS has on their library."

"Hold on." Shade brushed past Miles, giving Chaos a wide berth before squeezing his way onto the small porch with us. "*You're* the ones who trashed their library? Ginger died because of you."

The back of my throat heated as I blew out an irritated breath. We should have left him at home. "Boston didn't kill Ginger. Chrys did."

"We'll explain everything after we find Patrice. She's our first priority." Ember picked up a pinecone and tossed it at the ward. The magic fried it like an electric bug zapper, and it exploded into tiny pieces. "I hope you have black tourmaline and horehound in your bag."

I clenched my teeth. Chrys had burned up my favorite satchel, so I'd had to stock one of my old ones that wasn't nearly as comfortable on my shoulder. "I don't, and I doubt it would work. This spell is different. I'm sure she wouldn't have cast one she knows we can get through. We need to unravel it." I followed the trail of magic down the jamb and across the porch where it penetrated the ground.

"She's an earth witch," Chaos said, following my gaze. "Her magic originates in the land."

I hopped off the porch and brushed the leaves aside. "The ward gets its power from the earth here. It's not very old. Maybe we can dig it up. Neutralize the source."

Ember paced around the house, and the guys joined me on the ground. Wavering energy disappeared into the grass, but I had no idea how deep it went. Honestly, I'd had no idea how powerful Chrys was until today. She'd hid her magic well.

"I'm sure I can make it through." Chaos eyed the front door. "We survived the electrification ward."

"Did you not see what happened to that pinecone?" I shook my head. "No way."

"Let him," Shade said. "If he wants to blow himself to bits, I say go for it. Let him get vanquished."

I crossed my arms. "Except if he gets vanquished, I

die. This plot is deeper than you can imagine, so please just play along for now."

"Got shovels." Ember returned to the front yard, her arms full of gardening tools. "Patrice has a shed in the back." She dropped them at our feet.

Chaos picked up the biggest shovel and started to dig right over the magic.

"Wait." I grabbed his arm. "Dig around it, not on it. If you hit the spell, it will fight back."

He moved the tip of the shovel and planted it into the dirt. Five minutes later, we could see where the magic rooted, three feet deep. Gotta love demon strength.

"And?" Ember kneeled, cocking her head at the source. "Can we unplug it?"

"I think I can neutralize it." I set my satchel on the porch and rummaged through it for the ingredients. Angelica, basil, garlic, and a drop of myrrh oil would do the trick. I crushed and mixed the herbs before adding the myrrh. The potion popped and sizzled, turning to flakes like crushed red pepper.

I poured it into my hand. "We're all spent after what happened this morning, and who knows what we'll encounter inside."

"You may use my energy." Chaos held out his hand.

I looked from Shade to Miles. "This isn't the time to freak out over a demon. Believe me, he's the least of your worries right now." I slipped my hand into his.

Shade stiffened, his lids flying high, his brow shooting toward his hairline. "You can't."

Ember motioned for him and Miles to move back. "I don't like it any more than you, but she's right. We need to save our vim, so we're going to let her channel Chaos. She's done it before."

Shade's head moved back and forth so quickly, he probably didn't realize he was shaking it.

Miles nodded. "Do it. We can't let another witch die."

Chaos squeezed my hand, and a surge of demon power flowed into me, setting my nerves ablaze. I focused his chaos magic, channeling it into my being and casting my spell. "Uproot and end this magic source. Allow us to tread our intended course."

I dropped the flakes into the hole, and a pulse of energy shot out, whipping my hair back and stinging my cheeks. A high-pitched ring filled my head as ice flushed my veins. I rubbed my watery eyes, trying desperately to bring my vision back into focus.

"What just happened?" Ember asked.

I blinked, looking toward the house. The ward was gone. "I think that was an alarm."

"Indeed." Chaos ascended the porch steps. "She knows we're here, so we must move quickly." He disappeared into the house.

"Let's find Patrice and get out of here before she comes back." Ember followed him inside.

I slung my satchel over my shoulder and swallowed the dryness from my mouth before whispering a prayer to the goddess that we'd find our healer alive. Opening my senses, I inched forward, searching, feeling, trying to predict what might lie ahead. A current of dark magic ran over the remnants of Patrice's light, creating a choking sensation in my throat.

"It's thick in here," Miles said as he and Shade crept in behind me. "Fresh."

The foyer opened into a dining and living area. A wooden table with six chairs occupied the space to our left, and a blue sofa with white accent chairs stood to the right. Beyond that lay a kitchen and a short hallway with three doors.

Chaos came out from one of the rooms. "She isn't on this floor."

Ember appeared from another. "She's got a basement, right? I saw an entrance outside."

"Is she here?" Chaos asked me.

"We won't know unless we look." Shade went into the third room and returned to the hall. "Doesn't look like she has basement access from the inside."

"Is she here?" Chaos asked again.

I inhaled deeply and centered myself before searching the atmosphere for Patrice's energy. A tingle in my abdomen shot up to my head, pulling me into the kitchen.

"She's in the basement." A door stood closed between the fridge and the sink, and I opened it to find the pantry. Chaos stepped in behind me, and Ember wiggled past him.

"Is there a hatch in the floor?" She pulled a cord, turning on an overhead light, and stomped on the wood. "It sounds solid."

"It's here." I tugged one of the shelves, and the whole unit swung toward me, revealing a set of stairs. I cast my revealing spell. No magic blocked our descent, so I motioned for Chaos and Ember to take the lead.

"If you knew where the basement door was, why didn't you say so?" Shade came down behind me, with Miles on his heels.

"I didn't know."

Patrice's basement looked exactly how I imagined a healer's would. To the right lay the mundane: a washer-dryer, water heater, and furnace taking up most of the space. To the left stood a massive shelving unit filled with every kind of herb and oil imaginable. Mixing bowls, jars, and instruments lay atop a nine-foot, wooden table in front of the shelf, and more bundles of herbs and flowers hung from the ceiling, drying.

I walked past her workspace to the back of the

room. From the entry, the walls appeared to meet, ending the basement, but as I got closer, I found an opening around the corner that led into an unfinished space with a dirt floor. Whether it was a random optical illusion or built this way on purpose, I couldn't be sure, but it didn't matter. I'd found Patrice.

"Oh, my goddess." Ember rushed in and dropped to her knees before I could check for protection spells. Thankfully, nothing exploded when she touched our healer's forehead.

Patrice lay on her back in the dirt, a mess of roots crisscrossing over her body, pinning her down. Thick shoots covered her legs, stomach, and chest, while smaller sprouts crawled across the rest of her, creating a web around her that almost looked like a cocoon.

Ember grabbed a root in one hand, a dagger in the other. "Help me get her out."

"Wait." I paced toward my sister and clutched her shoulder. "Look." I gestured to webs pulsing softly against her skin. "If the roots are drawing out her energy, and we start hacking away at this setup, we could kill her."

Miles hung back in the doorway. "Is she..." He cleared his throat. "Is she alive?"

"I hope so." I kneeled next to Ember and studied our friend. She was a natural redhead and always pale, but her complexion had taken on a milky, ashy tone. Patrice lay utterly still, so I bent down, aligning my eyes with her chest. It rose and fell infinitesimally, nearly impossible to detect.

"I think she's breathing. You check." I moved so Ember could look.

"Yeah. It's shallow, but she's alive." She stood and dusted off her knees. "Anybody know another earth witch we could call for help unraveling this spell?"

"True elemental witches are rare," Chaos said. "Even more rare are those who don't run their own covens."

"Like Chrys." I walked around Patrice, following the patterns of the roots. There were too many of them for my uprooting spell to work, even with chaos magic giving me a boost. "She wants control of Salem."

"Elementals aren't the be-all, end-all." Shade squatted by Patrice and examined her condition. "This web isn't drawing nutrients from her. It's putting magic into her."

"How can you tell?" Ember bent down beside him.

He pointed. "Look at the direction of the pulses."

"They're moving toward her." She straightened and turned to me. "Chrys is using them to sedate her."

"She wants her alive," I said.

"And if the roots aren't drawing from her, ripping them apart won't kill her." She reached behind her back and unsheathed her sword.

I took a step backward. "Hack away."

With both hands, Ember raised the sword above her head and swung it down onto the biggest root, just above where it met the ground. The blade sliced halfway through, so she tried again, severing it with the second blow.

Miles grabbed the loose root and pulled, the webs dissolving as he yanked it away from Patrice's body. The ground shuddered, and the root Ember had cut shimmered, sprouting three tendrils where there used to be one. They snaked their way toward Patrice, and Miles sliced one with his dagger. Three more shoots grew from the cut.

"These roots behave like a hydra," Chaos said. "Cutting them will only make your healer's situation worse."

"Burn them," Shade said before cutting his gaze to me. "Ember, not you."

"Oh, that's right." I crossed my arms. "You slept through the whole ordeal. She makes them fireproof."

"We can try." Ember lit her sword ablaze and swung again. "Cauterize, bitch." The root sizzled, and three more grew in its place.

"Perhaps hellfire." Chaos gathered a flame in his hand and shot it at the base of the offending root. Heat blasted against my face, and if I wasn't fireproof, it would've singed my eyebrows. Lucky for Miles and Shade, they stood far enough away to avoid the brunt of it, but they both backpedaled into the wall behind them.

"What the hell?" Shade wiped the sweat from his brow and sneered at the undamaged root. "Are you trying to kill us all?"

"Just you," Chaos said so low only I could hear. "Your adversary is well-prepared against our power. Fire will not work."

"She couldn't have thought of everything." I rummaged through my spell kit, though I couldn't tell you what I was looking for. An idea. An inkling. Anything to get Patrice out of this mess. "My molasses spell got through her defenses. What else might she not expect?"

"Weed killer." Miles paced toward the exit. "The roots are charged with magic, but they're still roots."

"That's genius." Ember followed him out the door. A minute later, they returned with a gallon-sized jug of plant poison.

Miles poured it in a circle around Patrice, focusing on the biggest roots. With the jug empty, we gathered around, willing it to work its mundane magic. The smallest root by her left foot began to shrivel, the webs spinning out from it dissolving, and we held a collective breath. A few more webs retreated, but we'd need twenty gallons of the stuff to pry her loose.

"They're sucking the poison up into the plants above ground." Shade kicked the single shriveled one aside, freeing Patrice's foot. "Even if we had enough poison to kill whatever is making this trap, it would take days."

"Who's got another idea?" Miles asked.

Chaos huffed, and his mouth pinched. "It pains me to say this, but one of you can speed the killing along." He looked at Shade. "Plants require sunlight. Shadow extinguishes light."

"I don't think making it dark is going to kill this thing," Ember said. "Otherwise plants would die every time the sun sets."

Shade arched a brow at Chaos, his expression conspiratorial and not the least bit sour. "Shadow magic can do more than block light and conceal things."

My demon nodded. "It can draw light out, destroying the life it helped sustain."

Shade laughed once, like he couldn't believe what he was about to say, and he looked at me. "If you can pinpoint which plant she used to create this trap, I can kill it."

"What?" Ember stood next to me and crossed her arms. "Since when?"

"Since Chrys had me try. Come on." He walked out of the room, leaving us standing there, gaping.

Wait. What? Chrys had been coaching Shade on using dangerous magic. Who else had she gotten to?

"Go ahead," Miles said. "I'll stay with Patrice."

"What the hell, Shade?" Ember stomped up the stairs, with Chaos and me on her heels.

We followed him out of the house and into the yard before he explained. "She told me I was helping test her magic. She wanted to find a way to fight off dark magic with her earth powers in case we were ever under attack."

"When really she wanted to learn how to counter you." I rubbed my forehead. Were there any of us she hadn't fooled? "You weren't the least bit suspicious?"

He shrugged. "She never gave me reason to be."

She'd never given any of us reason to believe she was anything but kind, sweet Chrys. "Was she ever successful in countering you?"

"No." He lifted his head in pride. "I'd never dared tap into that side of my magic. Too many shadow witches end up going dark. But she convinced me it was for the greater good, so..." He lifted and dropped his shoulders again as if shrugging off any blame we might want to throw at him.

"Wow." Ember peered up at a tree. "Okay. Let's do it then. Which one is she controlling?"

I focused, centering myself and searching for the offending tree. Only, it wasn't a tree at all. The tug in my mind carried me to a rose bush in the flowerbed. "It's this one."

"This isn't the time for jokes." Shade turned

toward the maple. "There's no way that little bush is doing that much damage."

"It's not a joke, Shade." I parked my hands on my hips.

"You didn't even cast your little spell." He wiggled his fingers, mocking me.

Chaos stiffened, curling his hands into fists, and I patted his shoulder.

"She's developed our dad's power." Ember wrapped her arm around me. "She hasn't been wrong yet."

"If you want to kill a perfectly good tree, be my guest." I gestured to the maple. "I hope you'll have enough vim left for the real problem when you're through."

He narrowed his eyes, offense all over his face. Then he softened and walked toward me. "I won't have any vim left at all. It's the most taxing magic I've ever cast. This one, you said?"

I nodded.

"I'll be useless after this. Can I trust you to have my back?" He looked from me to Ember.

"We've got you," she said.

"You can trust us." I stepped back, giving him space to work his spell, lest he accidentally cast his shadow too far and suck the light out of me in the process. Chaos rested his hand on my back, and I leaned into his side, letting his warmth envelop me.

Shade took a few deep breaths, nodding as if either convincing himself he could trust us or that he could accomplish this feat. Maybe it was both.

He lifted his hands in front of his chest, and black smoke billowed between his palms. With his fingers outstretched, he widened his arms, the shadow magic growing between them. He whispered a spell, but I couldn't make out the words. The shadow stretched outward to the rose bush, cascading around it and enclosing it in darkness.

"How did you know he could do this?" Ember whispered.

"All shadow witches have this ability." Chaos slid his hand across my back to rest on my hip. "We're lucky he already knew how to use it."

The tendons in Shade's neck tightened. He groaned and then wheezed.

"Are you okay?" Ember called, and he gave his head a tiny nod.

Two full minutes passed before he let out a hard exhale and doubled over. We rushed to his side, and Ember and I helped him stand as the shadow rolled back into his chest. The rose bush shriveled and crumbled to dust.

We took Shade to the porch and lowered him onto the steps. Sweat dripped from his brow, and he heaved in a ragged breath. "Patrice?"

"I'll go check." I hurried inside and down the stairs

into the unfinished part of the basement. The roots around Patrice had crumbled, and Miles wrapped his arms beneath her shoulders, hauling her toward the exit.

"Let me help." I grabbed her feet, and we carried her out of the room.

The energy shifted, and I turned around. The air shimmered as a rift opened, and a set of long, thick talons pushed through.

"Well, crap."

# CHAPTER 2

# ASH

"Chaos!" I shouted as we positioned Patrice in a chair. "Ember, Shade, we need you."

Miles grabbed two knives from his shoulder harness and stormed back into the room. Patrice's head lolled to the side, so I pushed it upright, balancing it on the back of the chair. "Hang tight. We'll come back for you." I started for the unfinished room as my sister and my demon clomped down the stairs.

"What happened?" Chaos raced to my side. "Are you hurt?"

"Surprisingly, no. I've made it this far into our current adventure without a scratch." I stopped outside the entrance. "But there's a rift. Something nasty wants to come through."

"It's already through," Miles yelled before he grunted and his knife thudded on the ground.

"Get binding and sealing spells ready." Ember marched past me and followed Chaos into the room.

"What's happening?" Shade stumbled down the stairs.

"A rift. Wait with Patrice." I grabbed both potion bottles and stepped inside.

Chaos stood face to face with the fiend. It had a wide, pug nose, spiraling horns, and charcoal-colored skin, making its species unmistakable.

"Not this guy again." Ember stood two feet behind Chaos, clutching her sword in both hands. Miles rocked from foot to foot, gripping his knives so hard his knuckles turned white.

"Tell me that's not the same shedim we already vanquished." I stood back, giving them room to fight, but I was ready to mend the rift the moment they sent the bastard back through.

"It's not the same." Chaos stepped toward it. The fiend moved back.

"Holy mother of magic." Shade stood in the doorway, slumping against the jamb. "What is that?"

"It's a shedim." Chaos took another step forward. It moved back again.

"Bind it." Ember moved next to him. "I'll vanquish it."

"That won't be necessary." Chaos grabbed the

shedim by the neck and lifted it from the ground. It hung limp in his grasp, not even trying to fight back as he shoved it through the invisible rift. "You can seal it now."

"Wha…" My mouth hung open. Ember scratched her head, and Miles gaped at Chaos.

"That's it?" She sheathed her sword. "All this time, you've been able to just shove them back through?"

"When I don't have to hide my true identity, demons will not be an issue." The shedim's talons protruded through the invisible rift. "No," Chaos said before winking at me. "Bad demon."

I laughed. "I'll have to cast a perimeter location spell first to make sure I get it all. I can't see the rift." I grabbed the premade potion from my satchel.

"Let me." Miles held out his hand. "I'll locate; you seal. We should share the tax on our vim."

"Let the demon do it." Shade slid down the wall to sit on the floor. "He doesn't need to recharge like we do."

"Can you seal it?" Ember asked.

Chaos shook his head. "Not from this side, no. But I can share my magic with Ash to help her."

I wasn't sure I could handle another burst of adrenaline like that, so I handed the location spell to Miles. He uncorked it, releasing the smoke into the air and reciting the incantation. It billowed and gathered around a four-foot tear in the veil. After popping the top on the mending potion, I poured it over the tear and said the spell. The fibers of reality wove back together, and the energy in the room lightened. We all exhaled as if the weight pressing down on our chests finally lifted.

"What's going...?" Patrice said from the other room before a thud sounded, like a body smacking concrete. "Oof."

Shade's legs stretched across the doorway, so I stepped over him and ran to her side. "Oh, honey. Here." I held her shoulders and helped her sit upright.

She clutched her head, her eyes pinching like she had one helluva headache. "Chrys."

"We know." Ember paced to us, and we helped Patrice into the chair. "Tell us what to mix to heal you."

"There's a headache powder in the brown jar on the second shelf. That and twelve hours of sleep should do the trick."

"I'm so glad you're alive." Miles had Shade's arm over his shoulder, and he led him to the table, leaning him against it before letting him go. "What did she say to you?"

Patrice shook her head, squeezing her eyes shut. Chaos rested his hand on my back.

"We'll have time to talk when we get home." Ember brought a mug of water with dissolved headache powder to her. "Chrys knows we're here. We need to get home quickly, and then we'll discuss what we know."

"Home, where Chrys set up who knows what kind of wards." I took the mug from Patrice after she drank it and handed it to Ember. "I never thought to check what she'd done."

"You didn't think you had reason to," Chaos said.

"Let me grab a few necessities, and we can go." Patrice stood, took a bag from a cabinet, and filled it with herbs, oils, and powders before heading upstairs. We followed her up, and she took more vials and herbs from the kitchen. "I think I'm good."

"Pack some clothes," Ember said. "You're sleeping at our place for a while."

We waited in the living room as she packed, all of us silent, including Shade. When she finished, Chaos carried her suitcase to the car, while Miles helped Shade into the front seat. Ember drove to Miles's house and parked in the driveway.

"Do you have enough vim for one more revealing spell?" She twisted in her seat to face me. "We need to make sure his house isn't booby-trapped before we go inside."

"Yeah, I think so." I opened the side door and climbed out.

"I can assist you." Chaos followed me onto the pavement.

"Thanks, but I'm good." I had to use my demon's

magic sparingly. Too many rushes of power from him, and I might turn to the dark side too.

"What about me?" Shade asked. "My house and all my clothes are ashes now."

"We're the same size. I'll get enough of mine for both of us." Miles exited the van, leaving Patrice and Shade alone.

I rested a hand on Chaos's chest. "Will you wait here? They're defenseless right now."

He nodded and crossed his arms, widening his legs into a bodyguard stance.

I said the incantation. No magic protected Miles's home, so he opened the door. One last spell on the inside revealed nothing sinister. "Unless something is cloaking the nastiness, I think it's safe."

"Wait at the van." Ember clutched her sword just in case. "I'll go in with him."

"Gladly." Because my vim was nearly spent, and I still had to figure out what Chrys had done to our house. The twelve hours of sleep Patrice mentioned sounded like pure heaven. I climbed into the van, and Chaos stayed on guard duty until Ember and Miles returned with two giant duffel bags.

I rested my head on Chaos's shoulder on the short drive home, letting his warmth soothe me. He carried everyone's bags upstairs, leaving Patrice's in Cinder's room and Miles's in my parents'. Once we got everyone settled in the living room, I ordered three large pepperoni pizzas, gathered some supplies, and went with Ember to check the wards.

Outside on the sidewalk, Ember slipped her hand into mine, sharing her vim with me as I revealed what Chrys had done. Golden sparkles gathered around the perimeter of the building, coating the doors and windows.

My sister laughed, unbelieving. "She set up a ward to keep out the fae? That's it?"

"Apparently so." I rubbed oil on four railroad spikes and handed her two with a hammer. "You do the back, and I'll do the front."

"Sounds good." She headed to the back of the building, and I hammered a spike into the slim space where the cobblestone met the foundation. After placing the second one at the other corner, I joined her around back to cast our spell.

"Protect this space from malice and harm. If our ward is broken, we will be warned." We pushed our magic toward the building, hoping to wrap it in a cocoon of protection, but our spell hit a barrier and bounced back, stinging my cheeks and blowing through my hair.

"Oh, for Hecate's sake." I threw my hands into the air. "What the hell did you do, Chrys?"

A meaty hand landed on my shoulder, sending my heart into my throat. I squealed and whirled around, throwing a punch at the same time. My knuckles met Chaos's rock-hard chest, nearly crushing my bones.

"Ow! Son of a bison." I shook my hand. "You scared me to death."

"I require more clothing if I'm to blend in with your world." He gently gripped my fingers, brushing his over the tops before bringing them to his lips. "And we need to work on your self-defense skills."

Yes, my stomach fluttered. So what?

I tugged from his grasp and glanced at Ember. She gave me a reluctant nod and shrugged as if the simple movement of her shoulders wore her out. I understood exactly how she felt...

Spent.

"There's a store two blocks over." I laid my hand on his chest where I'd hit him. "I'll give you my card after you help us unravel whatever Chrys did to our building."

He peered at the roof before raking his gaze over the property. "I take it she did not cast a ward to keep out ill intent."

Plopping onto the back steps, I rummaged through my bag for supplies. "She put multiple layers on the building. The outermost is a ward to make sure we wouldn't suspect, but it's only to keep out the fae."

"The fae?" He arched a brow.

"Next is probably a cloak to hide whatever's

beneath it." Ember sat next to me and crushed the herbs I'd dumped into the bowl.

"We need to remove the ward first, and then we'll figure out the next layer, unravel it, and hopefully get to the final layer." I poured in the oil, and the potion sizzled.

"And you need my assistance to ascertain her spells?" Chaos placed his palm against the wall. "I feel dark magic, but I'm no witch. I can't tell you what hexes she cast."

"Not exactly." I stood and tugged Ember up. "We need to borrow your power to undo her darkness. We're running on fumes."

His brow furrowed. "Fumes?"

"We're tired and hangry," Ember said. "Whatever is underneath the ward fought back and wouldn't let us set up another one."

I tossed the potion onto the faery ward and held Chaos's and Ember's hands. My poor sister was as drained as I was, but as Chaos's demon magic flowed through me, I opened up and shared it with Ember.

She gasped. "Whoa."

"It's a rush, isn't it?" My entire body heated, especially my nether region, and I could only hope Ember didn't feel that part of Chaos's essence too. It didn't matter at this point. I just wanted to get our house protected so we could eat and crash.

Ember and I recited the undoing spell. Thankfully, the ward unraveled easily. We cast the magic-revealing spell, and it hit Chrys's cloak. Similar to the one Cinder had placed in her room, it fought back, sending out a pulse so strong it rattled in my chest.

I mixed up the next potion and blew the powder at the cloak before we joined hands again and spoke the incantation. I couldn't tell you if Chrys's spell was weaker than Cinder's, or if Chaos's power made us that much stronger, but the cloak dissolved, leaving only the final layer. Hopefully.

"Hold on. I need a break." Ember sat on the steps and rubbed her palms on her pants. "My nerves feel like they've been dipped in alcohol and rubbed with salt. How are you still standing?"

"Ash's magic counters mine," Chaos said. "She is the epitome of order. I believe the human expression would be 'she is the yin to my yang.'"

She pursed her lips and nodded. "I can see that."

"We can do the next one." Clutching my demon's hand, I recited the revealing spell one more time. Golden sparkles clung to the windows and doors, revealing an icky, sticky, dark magic hex.

"Good goddess." Ember stood and moved next to me.

"What is it?" Chaos asked.

"It's a..." I tilted my head, squinting at the magic. "It looks like a vim-draining spell. Or maybe not draining but making it hard to replenish. She's been keeping us weak." And that explained so much.

My sister's hoarse laugh sounded forced, and she crossed her arms, irritation evident in her tight expression. "How long do you think it's been here?"

I traced my gaze along the tendrils of the hex. "It's stuck on pretty well. See how it slips between the building and the cobblestone? She rooted it in the earth."

Ember sighed heavily. "Of course she did. And we can't dig it up without breaking the cobble and having the city on our asses."

"Maybe we don't need to. Wait here." I darted inside to the library and walked straight to the book I needed. I'd have to ponder how easy that was later. I returned to the back of the building and opened the book right to the spell I wanted. So friggin' easy!

Tracing my finger over the page, I read the list of ingredients while Ember retrieved them from my satchel. Basil, garlic, Solomon's seal. I crushed and mixed, and the potion puffed, a light blue cloud floating upward and spreading across the hex.

I laid the book on the top step and took their hands again.

"Hold on," Ember said. "Her hex fought back against our protection ward. What if it happens again?"

"We've got Chaos this time. We can neutralize it."

She pursed her lips and inhaled. "Okay."

We read the incantation in unison. Nothing happened, so we tried again. Still nothing.

"One more time," I said. "The power of three."

We recited the words, channeling Chaos and sending out as much magic as we could. My insides burned, and my nerves felt electric with all the demon power I channeled. Was it bad that I enjoyed the rush? Maybe, but we couldn't do it without his help. And this *had* to be done.

The building rumbled. A dark film stretched over the brick, pulling tighter and tighter and tighter until it popped and dissolved.

Chaos drew his magic back in, and I sagged against his side.

"Let's set up this protection ward before the adrenaline wears off." Ember tugged my hand, and I straightened.

We recited the incantation in unison once more. "Protect this space from malice and harm. If our ward is broken, we will be warned."

This time, the ward held. Thank the goddess.

Ember jerked from my grasp and rubbed her palm on her pants. "I hope to never need to do that again."

The sentiment wasn't the same, but I didn't tell her that. Instead, I tugged my credit card and house keys from my bag and handed them to Chaos. "Can I trust you to not cause any trouble?"

He fought a grin. "I will do my best."

"Straight to the store and back. Do not go rogue. Do not hurt or kill anyone." I tapped my finger against his chest. "That includes messing with their minds."

"You have my word." He winked and walked away while Ember and I went inside.

"Thanks for doing that," I said as I dragged myself up the steps.

"We didn't have a choice." She followed me up. "But seriously, sis. You can't keep channeling him. His power could be addictive, and with your curse still active..."

I waved off her concern. "I've got it under control."

"Do you?"

Good question.

## CHAPTER 3
# CHAOS

I returned from the clothing store to find a man holding three flat boxes and knocking on the front entrance door. He huffed and rang the buzzer, shaking his head before looking at his phone. His mouth drew downward, and lines creased his forehead.

"Are you the delivery person?" I approached with caution, opening my senses to detect any magic he might exude. I found none.

"I've been knocking for five minutes. Here." He shoved the boxes at my chest before stepping back and holding his hand toward me, palm up.

I'd seen plenty of people on the television return the gesture by slapping the outstretched palm, so I hooked the bags onto my fingers beneath the pizza boxes and "gave him five."

He scoffed, his attitude growing more fowl by the second. "My tip, man. What the hell's wrong with you?"

My eyes heated, the green undulating around my pupils. If I hadn't given Ash my word that I would harm no one, this delivery boy would be nothing more than a pile of soot. Instead, I straightened my spine and leaned toward him. "I suggest you treat your elders with respect. You never know what we're capable of."

His eyes widened, and his throat bobbed with his hard swallow. "Never mind. We're good."

I tilted my head slightly, and he took two stumbling steps backward before turning and running to his vehicle.

"Chaos! What did you do?" Ash stood in the doorway, her arms crossed over her chest.

"He insisted on a tip, so I gave him one." I shrugged and stepped inside. "I didn't use my power on him if that's what you're asking."

She arched a brow. "Did he have blond hair and a scar on his lip?"

"Indeed. And an attitude worse than Shade's."

"That's John. He's an ass." She locked the front door and led the way to the stairs. "Come on up. We're so hungry, we're about to eat our shoes."

"Surely you have something else to eat in your

kitchen. Leather is an animal product, but it's not for consumption."

She stopped and turned to me, laughing, her entire face lighting up with beauty. "It's an expression."

I couldn't help but smile. "Is it?"

"Well, if it isn't, I just made it one." She continued up the stairs.

In the kitchen, I set the boxes on the counter before taking my clothes to Ash's bedroom. When I returned, she handed me a piece of round, stiff paper and set three slices of pizza on it. With our plates full, everyone settled in the living room. Ash sank onto the sofa next to me, and our legs touched. Normally, she moved away when this happened, but not this time. She rested her shoulder against mine, and warmth filled my chest before a fist of dread squeezed it tightly.

This witch would never be mine. Not unless I took her to Hell with me, and I knew without a doubt that she would never leave her sisters. But perhaps, with a little convincing...

"It's time for answers," Shade said around a mouthful of food. "What's going on?"

"We should ask the same of you." Ash took two gulps of water and set her glass on the coffee table. "What the hell were you doing in our house, and why did you hit us with a nerve hex?"

He leaned forward in his chair. "I came here because you're harboring a demon. The spell was meant for him."

"What made you think I was a demon? You seemed surprised when you figured it out." I folded a slice in half and ate half in one bite.

"Chrys thought..." He clamped his mouth shut.

Chrys. He'd fallen victim to a dark witch's whims. Who was I to judge him for that?

Miles sat next to Patrice on the smaller sofa, his shoulders moving toward his ears. "Ginger told her we sensed something off in your house. Maybe she..." His eyes glistened, and he inhaled a shaky breath.

"Maybe we should start from the beginning," their healer said. "It sounds like we all have pieces to the puzzle that the others are missing."

Ember traded a glance with Ash. "Do you want to tell them, or should I?"

She set her empty plate next to her cup. "I will. It's all about me, anyway."

"You—" Shade began to quip, but he closed his mouth again.

Ash took a deep breath and straightened her spine. "I didn't break the curse on our coven. I *am* the curse."

She told them about Isabel's wrath, about how every High Priestess in the coven had lied about the curse and claimed a third-born daughter would die in infancy. Patrice watched her tell the story, sympathy creasing her forehead as she listened. Miles sat stoic, undoubtedly trying to hold back tears for his deceased girlfriend, and Shade's face pinched in his signature sour expression.

Ash shrugged, the sharp movement making her bounce on the cushion. "So our parents tried to find these guys and failed." She pointed her thumb at me. "Cinder figured out how to summon them and convinced Discord to take her across the veil to rescue Mom and Dad. I found the sigils and accidentally summoned Chaos into my mind. We retrieved his skull and got him out of my head, and now we need to get Mayhem's skull, which Chrys has."

Ember set her empty plate on the table. "Once we summon Mayhem, we can bring everyone back to this side of the veil, end the curse, and put everything right again. That's all we know. Who's next?"

"Hold on." Shade pinched the bridge of his nose. "If Cinder summoning Discord started the weakening of the veil, and Ash summoning Chaos made it worse, won't Mayhem tear it to shreds?"

"Your situation will get worse before it improves." I glanced at Ash's hands folded on her lap and fought the urge to hold them in mine. "However, once my brothers and I return to our realm permanently, the Holland sisters have the power to mend the veil. Everything will be as it was before."

"Except it won't." Miles stared at the half-eaten pizza on his plate. "Ginger will still be dead."

And I would live the rest of my existence knowing my perfect match could never be mine. The ache in my chest reached up to my throat.

"Miles." Ash shifted forward, leaning toward him. "I know it's hard to talk about, but do you think Ginger was working with Chrys?"

"I don't." He shook his head. "I mean, Chrys could have been the one who got her into dark magic, but Ginger would never hurt anyone."

"Why is Chrys even doing this?" Shade asked. "What does she want with Mayhem's skull?"

"My guess," Ember said, "is that she's working with Boston. She's either a member of their coven, or she's using their knowledge to try and take control of Salem."

Once again, Ember and I agreed. "That's a plausible explanation. It is rare for an elemental witch to be content without ruling."

Patrice nodded. "When she got to me, she said she wanted me alive because she'd need a good healer when she took over the coven."

"There you go," Ash said. "She knows about the curse. Hell, she and Cinder were close friends so it wouldn't surprise me if Chrys knew about her plans to free the demons and save me."

"And she's using it to her advantage," I said.

"Without Mayhem and Discord, I can't lift the curse on Ash."

"She's hoping Ash will do the dirty work and take out all the light witches for her." Ember stood and began pacing. "But you two." She pointed to Miles and Shade. "How did she get to you?"

Shade's brow slammed down over his eyes. "She manipulated us, convinced us to be suspicious. She's the reason I came here last night. I thought I was saving you, that you didn't know what he is, but when I saw Ash in bed with him, I lost it."

He flicked his gaze to Ash. "I'm sorry."

She flinched. "Umm. Thanks?"

"I don't know how she got the sigils onto us," Miles said. "I don't even remember her coming inside. I guess she used a binding spell?"

"A doozy of one," Ash said. "I could never have guessed how powerful she is. She fooled us all."

"What are our next steps?" Patrice rose and gathered the empty plates before taking them to the trash can.

Ember looked at me. "Do we let her summon Mayhem herself?"

"I don't think she can," Ash answered. "From what she said, it sounded like Isabel kept the sigils separate from the map. The book in our vault must've had the only copy."

"Can she summon him without the sigil?" Shade asked.

"Our marks are required for us to pass across the veil. She will either continue searching for the one you had, or she will look elsewhere. Isabel didn't create our marks. They've existed as long as we have."

Shade lifted his hands and dropped them in his lap. "She wants to take over Salem, and she's working with Boston. That much I follow, but why does she want to summon another demon? She knows it'll only make the veil weaker."

"Maybe that's part of her plan. Who knows how dark witches think?" Ash rolled her neck. "Besides, have you not seen how helpful Chaos is? Having a demon in her back pocket would level the playing field."

The only reason I'd been helpful to Ash was the bond I shared with her. I doubted my brother would feel for his witch the way I did about mine.

I was about to say as much when Patrice spoke, "Can I make a suggestion?"

"Please." Ember dropped onto the couch and pressed her fingers to her temples.

"We're all exhausted. No amount of healing I can provide will replace a full night of sleep." She clasped her hands in front of her chest. "I think we should rest and talk about our next steps in the morning."

"Yeah." Miles stood. "We'll be useless until morning. Let's get some sleep."

Shade drummed his fingers on the arm of the chair. "You can sleep with a demon in the house?"

Ash opened her mouth to speak, but Miles answered, "They set up the wards while he was outside. If he had ill intent, he couldn't have come back in." He turned and headed for the hall.

"Good night, everyone." Patrice followed.

I stood tugging Ash up with me. "No harm will come to any of you by my hand tonight."

"He means it," she said.

"You're safe here." Ember rose to her feet. "You can stay in our parents' room with Miles."

His face pulled into a frown. "I'm fine on the couch."

"Suit yourself." Ash led me to the hallway while Ember retrieved the same blanket and pillow she had offered me my first night here.

We stepped inside Ash's bedroom, and she closed the door, locking it before sliding her arms around my waist and resting her head against my chest. I held her tightly, pressing my lips to her hair and breathing in her intoxicating scent.

"I don't know why it is..." My shirt muffled her words, so she lifted her head and looked into my eyes. "But touching you always brings me a sense of calmness and safety."

I brushed a strand of hair from her forehead. "It's the bond we share."

"Your mark."

"No." I trailed my fingers down her cheek. Her skin felt as soft as down. "It's so much more than the ink on your arm. It's…"

"Fate?" She brushed her lips to mine.

"I believe it is." I moved my hand up her back to slide my fingers into her silky hair. "Do you?"

"I don't know what to believe." She stepped out of my embrace, and I immediately missed her warmth. "What I do know is that I'm in desperate need of a shower." Her tongue slipped out to moisten her lips as her gaze trailed down my body and up to my face. "Want to come wash my back?"

I inhaled deeply, the mere thought of seeing hot water rolling down her delicate skin making my dick twitch. "Your body requires rest."

"And I'll sleep so much more deeply if you help me relieve some of this stress. Don't you think?" She ran her finger down my abdomen, stopping at the top of my pants.

My stomach clenched. Who was I to deny her a restful night of sleep?

I removed my shirt and dropped it on the floor. "Lead the way, little witch."

She grinned and held up a finger. "Only if you

promise to be quiet. I don't have enough vim to cast a silencing spell."

I dropped my pants. "I will try my best."

Her gaze locked on my dick, and her pupils dilated as she stripped. Heat pooled in my groin, making my cock ache with need. She drew her bottom lip between her teeth and wrapped her fingers around my length, stroking it three times before turning and slinking into the bathroom.

I watched as she started the shower, testing the water with the inside of her wrist before stepping beneath the stream and beckoning me to join her. Water ran in rivulets over her shoulders, curving around her breasts and cascading down to her toes. She applied a floral-scented, liquid soap to a cloth and ran it over her face before turning her back to me and letting the water rinse her cheeks.

The view of her backside was as glorious as her front.

"Would you mind?" She handed me the cloth and moved her hair over her shoulder, giving me access to every dip and curve of her skin.

I did as she asked, cleansing her back before reaching around to her stomach. "I believe you missed a spot," I said into her ear, and her skin turned to gooseflesh.

"I believe you're right." She twisted in my arms and crushed her mouth to mine.

A growl rumbled in my chest, reaching upward to my throat as I coaxed her lips apart and tangled my tongue with hers. She fit in my embrace as if she were made for me, and the more time I spent with this witch, the more convinced I became that it was true.

Breaking the kiss, she trailed her tongue down my neck, nipping at my shoulder while her hands roamed over my chest. Her touch electrified me, sending flames of desire coursing through my veins. Pulling back to gaze at me, she grinned wickedly, one brow arching over a deep blue eye.

She ran one hand up to cup my cheek, while the other slid down to my stomach. I held in a groan as she inched her fingers closer to the prize, and when she wrapped her hand around my cock, stroking it like she owned it, I moaned.

"Bad demon." She stopped and squeezed me hard. "You promised not to make a sound."

I ground my teeth. "I promised to try my best."

"Try harder, or I'll have to send you to bed without your supper."

My eyes heated, the molten green of my irises undulating at her words. Not once in my entire existence had a lover told me what to do. I would never have obeyed if they tried, but this little witch...

I would do *anything* she told me to do.

I nodded, and she licked her lips before turning me

around, so the water hit my back. Then, she lowered to her knees.

Gripping my dick with one hand, she flicked out her tongue, swiping it over my tip. The sensation felt like warm velvet against my skin, and I let out a slow exhale. She did it again, this time circling her tongue around the head before sucking the first inch into her mouth.

I held my breath to stop my moan.

She looked up at me as she took me into her mouth as far as I could go, and she closed her eyes, drawing her head back, her teeth grazing my length before she released me. My knees nearly buckled when she took me back in. She released me again, looking up and running her tongue from the base to my tip.

My nostrils flared, and I reached down, hooking my finger under her chin and guiding her to her feet. She smiled and ran her hands up my body, tracing the cuts of my muscles, her fingertips memorizing my form.

"Your body is exquisite." She rose onto her toes, brushing a kiss to my lips. "Take me to bed."

Her whisper made me shiver. I shut off the water and grabbed a towel, wrapping it around her back, my length pressing against her stomach as I drank her in. She cupped my face, returning the passion in our kiss before pulling away and grinning. "Now, please."

A primal grunt rumbled up from my core, but I squelched it before it passed my throat. Scooping her into my arms, I carried her to the bed and lay her on the mattress, but she rose to her hands and knees, slinking backward like a cat.

"I love it when you look at me like you want to devour me." She nodded toward the empty space on the bed. "Lie down."

I did as I was told, lying on my back and fighting the urge to throw her down and take her. She wanted to be in control this time, and I would relinquish it to her for as long as she wanted it tonight.

She crawled toward me, straddling my hips and rubbing her slit over the length of my dick as she kissed me. Every muscle in my body tensed. I wanted to groan. To tangle my fingers in her hair and make her scream my name.

"Mmm..." she said softly against my lips. "Good demon."

Rising onto her knees, she guided me to her folds and took me in slowly, inch by inch until nothing separated us. She was tight and wet, and as she rose up and down my length, I couldn't tear my gaze away from her beauty.

Her lips parted, her breath quickening as she rode me. Grabbing my hands, she placed them against her breasts and closed her eyes, her expression one of sheer ecstasy as I caressed her.

"Oh, Chaos," she whispered and moved one of my hands down her body.

I pressed my thumb to her clit, and she gasped. Her rhythm increased, and she opened her eyes, biting her bottom lip and leaning forward to rest her hands on my chest. My entire body hummed with the need to feel her release.

I circled her sensitive nub, bringing her closer and closer to the edge until she pressed her lips together and moaned. She rode me hard and fast, tossing her head back as she found her release. I gripped her hips, holding her still and pounding into her, the orgasm twisting in my core, threatening to burn me alive if I didn't release it.

But I waited. I continued thrusting into her until she inhaled deeply, pinning me with her deep blue gaze and nodding her approval. I thrust two more times and let go. Ecstasy exploded inside me, rolling through my body like wildfire and setting my soul ablaze.

Panting, she collapsed on top of me, sliding her arms beneath my shoulders and holding me tightly. I traced my fingers up and down her back, reveling in the feel of her wrapped around me, of her body still one with mine.

"Never in my life has sex been this good," she whispered.

"We were made for each other, little witch."

"Mmm... It feels that way sometimes." She rolled to her side and snuggled against me.

For me, it felt that way all the time. Ash was the light to my darkness. The order to my madness. The one I wanted to spend eternity with.

My chest pinched with agony. There had to be an answer. Fate would not lead me to her and then tear her from my arms. I would do anything to spend my existence with her, no matter what the cost. It didn't matter what I had to do...

Ash would be mine.

# CHAPTER 4
# ASH

Voices and dishes clanking roused me from sleep, and I squeezed my eyes shut, willing myself back under. I lay on my side, the heat of Chaos's body against my back making me feel safe, cozy even.

A month ago, if you'd told me I'd be in bed with a demon, I would have laughed and called you cuckoo. Yet, there I was, wrapped in his strong embrace and enjoying every minute of it.

"The others are up." His deep voice, raspy from sleep, made me shiver in a good way.

I turned toward him, snuggling into his arms, my head fitting perfectly beneath his chin. "Tell me this is all a bad dream."

"If it were, I wouldn't be here."

"Tell me everything except you is a bad dream." I

closed my eyes, breathing in his warm, spicy scent. "I just want it all to go away."

Five seconds passed before he responded. "I can make it go away."

I laughed. "Without killing everyone."

Another long pause, and he kissed the top of my head. "Come to Hell with me."

I laughed again.

"I'm not joking."

I pulled back to see his face. He looked as serious as could be.

"We're meant to be together, Ash." He held my gaze with emotion-filled eyes. "We don't need my brothers to end your curse when I can take you away. Your coven will be safe if you're in Hell with me, and we can be together forever."

"You can't be serious." I scooted away, my brow furrowing. Surely he didn't think that was a viable solution.

"It would solve all your problems." He reached for me, but I rolled away and got out of bed.

"It most certainly would not. Too much sugary cereal has affected your brain. I'm not going to Hell with you." I opened my drawers and put on a bra and underwear.

He sat up, the sheets falling away from his statue-perfect body, and I fought the urge to shut him up by sitting on his face. Why did he have to be so frigging hot? I turned back to my drawers and shoved my legs into a pair of black pants.

"Why not?" He stood, all his glorious nakedness taunting me.

"The fire and brimstone, for one thing." I threw on a fireproof black shirt and wrapped a corset around my waist, hooking it in the front.

"It's not as bad as you think." He pulled on his jeans. "We could be happy there."

"I could not be happy in Hell." I fumbled with the ribbons in the back of my corset as he finished dressing. "I'm not leaving my sister or my coven no matter how hot a fire you light in my core. What is wrong with this damn thing?" It wouldn't tighten the way it was supposed to.

Chaos moved behind me and took the ribbons, pulling and tugging until it tightened perfectly. "You're meant to be mine."

"Whoa." I turned to face him. "I thought we agreed we'd have a little fun when we could, and then you'd go home and I'd stay here. That was the deal."

"I'm not sure I can exist without you." The sincerity in his eyes nearly buckled my knees, and Ember's words echoed in my mind.

*What if he falls in love with you? What if you fall in love with him?*

Hell, no. That wasn't happening. I couldn't let it. "Let me make this very clear. I am *not* going to Hell with you or anyone else, so get that idea out of your head right now."

He looked at me silently as I put on my socks and boots. Maybe sleeping with a demon wasn't such a good idea after all.

"I hear your words." He opened the door and walked out of my room.

He heard my words? Was he implying that I didn't mean what I said? If so, he didn't know me as well as he thought he did. I'd always been a *say what I mean and mean what I say* gal.

I joined the others in the kitchen. Shade cut his gaze from Chaos to me, but thankfully he kept his mouth shut. It was too early in the morning to deal with his bullshit. Patrice stood at the stove, frying bacon, and Miles took two slices of bread from the toaster, adding them to the stack, while Ember poured two more cups of coffee, offering them to Chaos and me.

I accepted the mug and sank into a chair at the table. "Where'd all the food come from?"

"Miles and I stepped out this morning and went to the corner market." Patrice added four more slices to the pan. They sizzled and popped, filling the room with their delicious aroma and making my mouth water.

Patrice plated the food and presented us with a spread of scrambled eggs, bacon, and toast with jam before joining Chaos, Ember, and me at the table. Miles and Shade sat at the counter, and we ate in glorious silence. When we finished, I collected the empty plates and carried them to the kitchen. Chaos picked up a dish towel and joined me at the sink.

"I've got it." I snatched the towel from his hands.

He grabbed it back. "You wash; I'll dry."

I gritted my teeth. "I was planning to put them in the dishwasher."

He stepped away and opened it, gesturing to the racks already full. Dammit, I'd forgotten to empty it.

Shade clutched his coffee in both hands. "Are we not going to talk about the fact that Ash is sleeping with a demon?"

Ember refilled her mug and leaned a hip against the counter. "It's irrelevant to our problems, so no. We're not going to talk about my sister's sex life."

Hallelujah.

I finished washing the dishes and poured the last of the coffee into my mug. "We have two options. We can wait it out, let Chrys find the sigils and summon Mayhem, and then hope Chaos can get to him before she uses him to destroy us. Or, we can go on the offensive."

"Being offensive is our best bet." Chaos dried his hands on a towel and dropped it on the counter.

I hung it in its proper place. "You don't even know—"

"We find her, kill her, and take the skull." He said it matter-of-factly, as if it were the only viable course of action.

"She nearly killed all of us," Miles said. "That won't be an easy feat."

"And good luck finding her," Ember added. "Scrying for Shade took so much vim we didn't have enough left to fight."

I blew out a long, slow breath and pressed my lips into a line.

"That's not what you meant, is it? You prefer to wait it out?" Patrice carried the frying pan to the sink and washed it. At least *someone* wanted to hear my suggestion.

"No. If she gets control of Mayhem, who knows what she'll do. We can't let her summon him." I sipped my coffee, waiting for them all to look at me. "We have to do it first."

"How?" Ember asked. "We don't have the sigils either. They burned up in Shade's house. Do you remember what they look like?"

"Not exactly, and we can't risk doing it wrong. Who knows what might happen if we did." I drummed my fingers against my mug and flicked my gaze to Chaos. "Can you draw them?"

His brow furrowed. "I believe so."

"That didn't sound convincing." Ember opened a drawer and pulled out a pad of paper and a pencil.

"I've never tried." He took the paper and gripped the pencil in his left hand. "Mayhem's mark is similar to mine, so it would start with a curve at the top." He laid the pad on the counter and began to draw.

I sipped my coffee and watched the sigil take form. The treble clef shape looked like Chaos's mark, but Mayhem's had sharper edges and more straight lines. When he got to the bottom, he looped it around to the right and paused.

"I think it goes left." I set my mug on the counter and pointed to his mistake.

"It most certainly goes right. What comes after this loop is why I paused. Mayhem and Discord have the same angles here, but they are reversed. I can't remember which is which."

"Well, that's a problem." I crossed my arms. "And I still think it goes left."

"It goes right."

"It doesn't matter." Ember tore the page from the pad and tossed it in the trash. "If neither of you remembers exactly, we're screwed. We'll have to get another copy of them."

I leaned against the counter. "Prince of Hell sigils won't be easy to find. If they were, Chrys would have them by now."

"If anyone can locate them, it's you." She returned the pencil to the drawer.

"Say you do find them," Shade said. "Then what? We still don't have the skull."

Chaos leaned against the counter next to me, and I fought the urge to scoot away. I was still miffed at him for the way he acted this morning, and miffed was good. It was better than the alternative, anyway.

*What if you fall in love with him?* No, no, no.

"One step at a time." I paced to the opposite end of the kitchen. "Chrys is looking for the sigils. We need to find them first, and then we can work on locating her and the skull."

"How will we find them first?" Miles asked. "She's probably been searching the witchy web since she figured out who Chaos is. That's a big head start."

"Chrys is just an earth witch." Ember wrapped her arm around me, giving me a side hug. "We've got a librarian on our team. Ash can find anything."

Finally a task I was confident I could handle. "Give me an hour. If there's a copy of those sigils somewhere on this continent, I'll find it." I headed for the stairs.

Chaos followed me down to my office, and I huffed, plopping into my squeaky chair. He needed to learn how to read the room. "I don't need any help."

He stood next to my desk, his gaze traveling from my eyes to my fists clenched on the surface. "I've upset you."

"Whatever gave you that idea?" I fired up my laptop, hoping to Hecate it still worked after Shade threw it on the floor. The familiar start-up ping sounded, and I let out a breath. *Thank you, goddess.*

"I assume your question was rhetorical." He picked up the drawers Chrys had pulled out and returned them to their rightful places in my desk.

Another sarcastic comment rolled through my mind, but it didn't make it past my lips. We didn't have time for games. If I wanted to keep this demon on my team, I needed to be straight with him. "You freaked me out up there."

"I didn't mean to."

A hairband sat loose on the edge of my desk, so I grabbed it and tied my hair into a bun. "I know you didn't, but..." I blew out another breath. "I like you a lot, but my loyalty lies with my coven. Going to Hell with you is not an option, and the fact you even suggested it is a huge red flag."

He rested his fingertips on my desk. "The suggestion was harmless."

"No, actually, it wasn't. I told you 'no,' and you implied that my 'no' didn't mean 'no.' That's not cool."

"I see." He clasped his hands and said nothing more.

I guess expecting yet another apology from a demon was asking too much. When he didn't offer one, I pulled up the witchy web and began my search. Looking for the demons' names didn't help. Chaos,

Mayhem, and Discord were normal words, and all I got were definitions and listings for the Discord social media site. I tried *prince of hell, demon prince sigil,* and a few similar search times, but those gave me paranormal romance novels written by witches. Believe it or not, only a handful of magical authors wrote stories about magic. Most paranormal romance writers were human. Go figure.

"Does your Higher Power not monitor searches like this?" Chaos leaned down, resting one hand on the back of my chair and the other on the desk. "Will you and your coven not be investigated for looking up demons?"

"I use an encrypted browser, and there isn't enough magic in the world for them to constantly spy on every coven's activity. We're fine." I swiveled my chair, and he straightened, stepping back. Maybe a reverse image search would bring better luck. I grabbed my phone and snapped a photo of the mark on my arm before uploading it to my laptop.

Twenty minutes later, I'd found nothing. I slumped in my chair while Chaos returned the books Shade had knocked down to the shelves. "You don't have to do that," I said. "When this is all through, I'm going to reorganize the whole library."

He put another book on the shelf. "The disarray bothers you, and this part of it was my fault."

I pursed my lips. How could he be such a brute and

then turn around and do something thoughtful? So annoying. "Thank you. I've exhausted the witchy web. Either we had the only copy of those sigils, or whatever book they might be in isn't listed."

He placed another volume on the shelf. "Was your dark grimoire listed?"

I dropped my head back on the chair. "No. Any coven who understands how powerful you are would hide it. Damn." I should have realized that before I even tried.

"If you can't find a copy, I doubt Chrys can either." He sat on the edge of my desk. "We should kill her."

And the brute was back. I pinched the bridge of my nose. "We don't kill people...on purpose."

"We should accidentally kill her."

I laughed, but I doubted he was joking. Then it hit me. "Hold on." I sat upright. "Magical beings would understand how dangerous summoning a Prince of Hell can be, but humans wouldn't. Your sigils could be sitting in a book in the Salem library, right under our noses. Let me check."

My fingers flew across the keys, my heart sprinting in my chest. Why hadn't I thought of this before? It took a few different search strings to get it right, but ten minutes later, there it was. "*The Complete Encyclopedia of Demonic Legions as recorded by Father Timothy Carson.*"

"Mortals keep an encyclopedia of my kind?" He

leaned closer to the screen and read the description. "'Explore the hierarchy of Hell from Lucifer down to the smallest fiends. Includes sigil artwork for each demon and summoning precautions.' Hmm. Sounds promising."

"It better be. It's the only thing I can find that comes close to what we need, and there's only one copy on record in all of North America." I opened another tab and searched the title on the web. No hits returned for this continent, but one came back from France.

"Is it in Salem?"

"Sadly, no. It's in New Orleans." I returned to the library site and clicked the entry. "And it's classified as a reference book, so we can't get it through interlibrary loan."

"Is New Orleans far?"

"Fifteen hundred miles. I'll have to fly there." I closed the laptop and shoved it into its case.

"You..." Chaos straightened, confusion pinching his features. "You have the ability to fly?"

"In an airplane, yeah." I rose and paced to the stairs. "What? Did you think I meant on my broom?"

"Of course not." He followed me up the steps. "But you made it sound as if you had an ability I was unaware of."

"There's a lot you don't know about me." I opened

the door to find Ember and the others packing up to leave. "What's going on?"

"Higgins called about another rift." She handed me my bag. "What did you find?"

"There's a demonic encyclopedia with sigil artwork in New Orleans." I set my satchel on the counter. "It's in the public library."

"Is it legit?" Miles asked.

"I'll have to go there to see. It's in the reference section."

"So they won't let you check it out." Ember tapped her foot. "You'll have to steal it."

My stomach clenched at the idea of stealing from a library, but she was right. If the book was legit, it needed to be held under lock and key, not sitting out available for anyone to play with.

"If Chrys hasn't already taken it," Shade said. "She's smarter than you think."

I rolled my eyes and swiped open my phone to bring up the New Orleans Public Library website. I clicked the number and pressed the speaker button.

It rang three times before someone answered. "New Orleans Public Library. How can I help you?"

"Hi. I'm calling about one of your reference books. It's called *The Complete Encyclopedia of Demonic Legions as recorded by Father Timothy Carson*. Do you still have that?"

The sounds of a keyboard clicking filled the silence. "Yes, ma'am. It's in our catalog."

"She could have stolen it already," Shade whispered. "They might not know it's gone."

I nodded. "Yeah, I saw it there online, but would you mind checking to see if you still have it in your possession? I'm going to travel a long way to look at it, and I'd hate to make the trip if it was transferred to another building."

"Hold please." Jazz music blasted through the speaker, so I turned down the volume. Five minutes later, she returned to the line. "Yes, ma'am. It's in the reference section on the second floor."

"Thank you." I pressed End and returned the phone to my pocket...without making a face at Shade, thank you very much.

"Good." Ember grabbed her keys from the peg. "Take Chaos with you. We'll hold down the fort until you get back."

"I can go alone. It's just a library." I needed to put as much distance as possible between us. His whole *I can't exist without you; you're meant to be mine* speech still had me reeling.

"I won't leave you unprotected," Chaos said.

I whirled to face him. "I've done just fine without you for twenty-four years. I don't need protection."

"Yes, you do," Ember said. "Sorry, sis, but the circumstances have changed. We're on the buddy system from now on, and you're the only person he listens to. Whatever lovers' quarrel you're having needs to end right now."

"Okay." I threw up my hands in surrender. "Take the premade spells from my kit. I'll put together some more before I...we...leave."

Patrice held up her phone. "There's a flight out of Boston in three hours. Do you think you can make it?"

Ember looked at the screen. "She can. Book it for her and Shade. Here's my card."

"Shade is not accompanying us." Chaos crossed his arms.

Honestly, I'd almost rather have gone with Shade at that point, but I knew what my sister meant. "You're going to use his ID, or they won't let you on the plane."

"Whoever *they* are, they can't stop me."

I opened my mouth to argue but thought better of it. Instead, I turned to Shade and held out my hand.

His expression pinched, growing even more sour, but he took his driver's license from his wallet and handed it to me. "Don't let him tarnish my name."

"No promises," I grumbled and gave it to Chaos. "I'll cast a glamour spell on the photo to make it look like you. When we're at the airport, your name is Shade."

He peered at the license before sliding it into his back pocket. "Understood."

"The flight is booked," Patrice said. "The return trip is tomorrow evening, but you can always change it if you need more time. I'm sending the boarding passes now."

Ember pulled me into a tight hug. "Don't forget to book a room and try to stay away from other witches."

I laughed and pulled away. "You do realize we're going to New Orleans, right?"

"Do your best to stay off their radar. Fire and water don't mix."

"I will."

Ember and the others left, leaving me alone with Chaos. I looked at him, and he looked at me, and for the first time since I'd met him, awkwardness expanded between us.

I didn't like it.

Not at all.

# CHAPTER 5
# ASH

I left two days' worth of bottled spells on the counter before we headed to the airport. At least, I hoped it would last two days. Between the rifts, Chrys, and Boston trying to get revenge for their library—if that was even why they were involved —I had my doubts. But they had Patrice now, and Miles was good at spell work. They'd be fine without me.

Hell, they might even be better off. Hecate knew their lives would be a helluva lot easier if I'd never been born. I lowered my gaze to my hands clasped in my lap. Chipped black polish partially coated my nails, which irritated me almost as much as the disarray in my library. I picked a piece off my thumb and flicked it to the ground.

A pair of black boots came into view in front of me,

and I lifted my head. Chaos handed me a cup and sank into the chair next to me. Our flight boarded in twenty minutes, so I'd sent him on a coffee run to give me some space.

"I was hesitant to try this concoction you call a pumpkin spice latte, but I'm glad I did. It's decadent." He pressed the cup to his lips and tipped it, closing his eyes as he sipped. "It's only available during this time of year?"

"That's part of what makes it so good." I took a drink and lowered the cup to my lap, toying with the paper sleeve. "What's it like in your realm?"

"I'm not sure anymore. It's been centuries. Why do you ask?"

"What was it like before you were imprisoned? Where did you sleep?" I cut my gaze toward a man practically yelling into his phone. Would it be bad of me to cast a silencing spell on him? If I were only doing it for myself, yes, it would. But, surely, I wasn't the only person who wanted to throw his phone across the room. Maybe for the greater good...

"In my realm, I don't require sleep. Otherwise, it isn't all that different from here. The only humans there are those who sold their souls into torture, but we have food and drinks, games, and entertainment. I assume it hasn't changed."

I peeled apart the insulating sleeve and dropped it into my lap as a sickening sensation formed in my stomach. "Are my parents and Cinder being tortured?"

He inhaled deeply, going silent for a full three seconds. "I don't know."

I set my cup and the ruined sleeve on the table next to me. "They're in Hell because of me. If they're being tortured, it's my fault."

"No." He clutched my hand.

"Yes." I pulled from his grasp. From the moment I possessed myself, my life had been nothing but go, go, go. Adrenaline rushes, vim depletion, danger, sex, exhaustion, sleep. This was the first time I'd had downtime in weeks, and sitting there in the airport, waiting to get on a plane, my mind finally had a moment to contemplate how much of a mess I'd made of my family, my coven, my town.

He set his cup on the floor at his feet and rested his hands on his knees. "Your family is in Hell because of the choices they made."

"Choices they wouldn't have *had* to make if not for me." I stared at the man yelling across the way, willing him to end the effing call for goddess's sake. The woman next to him huffed, glaring at him as she gathered her carry-ons and moved to the next row.

"Ash..." Chaos angled toward me.

"Screw it." I whispered a silencing spell and directed my magic at the cacophonous culprit. He yelled a silent *hello* a few times into the phone before shouting *can you hear me* twice. Jabbing his thick finger onto the screen, he ended the call, looked at the teenager next to him, and spoke, but no sound emanated from his lips.

"Freak." The teen scoffed and moved two aisles away.

"Maybe you're right." I turned to Chaos. "Maybe I should go to Hell with you. I could trade places with them. I stay, and they go home. My mom can help my sisters mend the veil from their side. I'm not there to destroy them all." I shrugged. "It makes sense."

He shook his head. "It's not a viable solution, and I never should have suggested it."

They called our flight for boarding over the speaker, so I stood and slung my bag over my shoulder. "I cause nothing but trouble everywhere I go. C'mon. Let's see what kind of mess we can make of New Orleans."

Patrice had booked us on a budget airline with no assigned seats. The man I'd hexed sat in the second row, and I whispered an undoing spell as I passed, moving to the back of the plane, as far away from him as possible. I found an empty row and scooted in, claiming the window seat. Chaos took the middle, leaving the coveted aisle seat empty. A woman saw the free space and made her way toward us, but when her gaze locked on Chaos, she swallowed hard and turned around to find another seat. The same thing happened with a man in a suit and a teenage boy in a hoodie.

I elbowed Chaos. "Are you doing something?"

"Just giving us privacy so we can talk freely."

I wanted to argue it was rude, but I had to admit if I could warn people away without wasting my vim, I'd do it all the time. "If the flight's full someone will have to sit there."

Thankfully, it wasn't full. I shoved my bag beneath the seat in front of me and buckled my seatbelt. "Do not, under any circumstances, use your chaos magic on this plane. No fire either."

"What is the purpose of a seatbelt? If the plane falls from the sky, I doubt remaining in our seats will provide safety." He buckled up and angled his body toward me.

"Sometimes there's turbulence. The plane will hit pockets with different air pressure and jerk down and up. Seatbelts keep us from falling all over the place."

The plane took off, and Chaos watched the world fall away through the window, his eyes full of wonder. His lips curved upward into an adorable smile, and he leaned closer, looking all around. "Humans have evolved so much since I was imprisoned."

"I'm not sure evolved is the right word. Our technology has grown by leaps and bounds, but we're not any better at being human beings. People still suck."

"You consider yourself human?" He leaned back in his seat and looked at me.

"Yeah. I mean, aside from having some magical abilities, witches aren't much different than humans. We're mortal, we exist in their world, hold their jobs, play their games, follow their laws. Most of us do, anyway."

He sighed. "You wouldn't be happy in Hell."

"Then why did you insist I come? Because that's starting to sound like the best thing I could do for my coven."

He leaned his head against the seat and closed his eyes. "Because I'm selfish. It's my nature to take what I want without regard to how it affects others."

"So you thought you could take me, whisk me away from my family, and keep me for yourself, never mind how I might feel about it." I shook my head. This right here was why I needed to keep my feelings for him in check.

He opened his eyes and pinned me with his gaze. "The thought crossed my mind, yes. Many times. I would raze the world to keep you safe."

Dammit if my stomach didn't flutter. "I don't want you to raze the world. As dysfunctional as it is, it's my home. I like my life in Salem."

"I know. That's why I never should have suggested you come to Hell. I will have to figure out another way to make you mine."

I laughed. "Good luck with that."

He lifted one shoulder. "Besides, even if we could find your parents and sister and release them, Mayhem would still be trapped. Chrys would find a way to summon him, and your coven would be destroyed."

"And I can't let that happen." I slid the window cover down, blocking the blinding light shining through.

"You won't. You're the only one who can defeat the earth witch."

I laughed a little harder. "You're still a funny little demon."

He arched a brow. "Nothing about me is little. I think you're aware of that."

"No kidding." Heat flushed my cheeks, and I shifted in my seat. Holy Hecate, how could a simple raised brow get me hot and bothered?

He leaned his left elbow on the armrest. "Chrys underestimates you. Everyone except Ember does."

"They just know what a magical klutz I am. They've seen me flub more times than they can count." I waved a hand flippantly. They knew what I was and wasn't capable of, and they were right to judge me for it.

He pursed his lips. "You underestimate yourself as well."

I shrugged. "I know my limitations."

"You limit yourself. If you had more confidence, you could be the most powerful witch in your coven."

"That's the thing though." I twisted toward him. "I don't care about power. I'm happy in my library and my studio. Ink is my jam."

He nodded. "I'm sorry for upsetting you this morning."

I searched my heart for a reason to stay mad at him, but I couldn't find one. Chaos was a demon. I couldn't expect him to behave like a human man. Hell, he actually behaved better than a lot of men. My brain couldn't find a logical reason to stay miffed either. For once, my heart and mind agreed on something.

"You're forgiven."

He took my hand, and this time, I let him hold it. I liked Chaos a lot. Too much, honestly, but knowing our relationship had an expiration date made it okay in my mind. He would leave me in the end, but first, he would save me.

My chest tightened, and an ache spread through my body. My heart didn't want him to leave. My brain told me he had to, but I would deal with that pain when the time came. For now, I would enjoy being wanted, because it sure as hell felt good.

We landed at Louis Armstrong Airport at six in the evening, right when the library closed. Since breaking and entering wasn't on my to-do list, we gathered our bags and took an Uber to our boutique hotel in the

French Quarter. The two-story building sported yellowish-beige paint with white trim, and a wrought iron fence that looked like cornstalks surrounded the property.

After checking in, Chaos carried the bags and we headed upstairs to our room. A king-size bed in an antique frame sat next to the window, and a matching armoire stood against the wall across from it.

Chaos sat on the edge of the mattress and ran his hand over the duvet. "I do hope we can make use of this tonight."

My stomach fluttered again, and heat pooled below my navel. We could make use of it right then and there if I wasn't famished. "If you're a good demon, maybe we can."

The green in his eyes rippled like water disturbed by a pebble. "I'll be very good."

Sweet spirits, was it hot in here? I grabbed my satchel and slung it over my shoulder. "Food first. I'm starving."

We left the hotel and made our way down Royal Street in search of a restaurant. Tourists milled about, and music and laughter from a block over filled the air. It was warm out...almost muggy...which was odd to a girl from Massachusetts. I pulled up my sleeves and tied my hair into a ponytail.

"This city is thick with magic. Not all of it is good." Chaos rested his hand on the small of my back.

"I know. New Orleans is like a beacon for the supernatural. A lot of vampires and shapeshifters live here, along with three different classes of witches." I found a restaurant, and we went inside. The scents of Cajun spices filled the air, making my mouth water.

We sat at a table by the window, and Chaos looked at me over his menu. "Light and dark witches. What's the third?"

"Voodoo. It's a lot like witchcraft, but they have their own spirits called loa. They have different rituals and beliefs, but they tap into the same energy from the universe as witches."

"Fascinating."

The server arrived to take our order, and I asked for the sampler platter with red beans and rice, etouffee, and jambalaya. Chaos ordered the biggest steak they had and a bottle of wine.

When the server filled our glasses and walked away, I took a sip of cabernet. It was bold and dry, and it warmed me from the inside out. Kind of like the man sitting across from me.

I set the glass down and let out a long sigh. "It feels so good to take a break. I kinda feel bad for Ember though. She's out there fighting monsters and sealing rifts, and I'm sitting in a French Quarter restaurant, enjoying a glass of wine with the hottest man on the planet."

"Something tells me Ember enjoys fighting." He picked up his glass and took a sip.

I laughed. "Oh, she definitely does. Maybe not this often, but fighting is in her blood."

"And ink is in yours. You all have something useful to contribute to your coven, and we are here, enjoying a glass of wine, because your skills require us to be here. Guilt is a useless emotion. You should let it go."

"I would if I could." Our food arrived, and I dug in. I'd been to New Orleans once before, but like most people in their early twenties in this city for the first time, I'd let the good times roll and drank more than I ate.

I shoveled a spoonful of etouffee into my mouth, and it was a spicy, savory flavor explosion on my tongue. Every bite of every morsel tasted almost orgasmic. Chaos nodded his appreciation with each cut of meat he ate, and we devoured our meals more quickly than a newbie in a maximum-security prison.

"That was so good." I reluctantly pushed my plate away. "I can't eat another bite."

"May I?" He picked up his fork.

"Have at it." I downed the rest of my wine and took a sip of water.

After paying the tab, we walked down Royal, looking in the shop windows and acting like a normal couple in a normal world, which was weird as weird could be. The shroud we put on his aura hadn't faded, so no one had a clue a Prince of Hell walked among them.

"Where is the music coming from?" he asked.

"Bourbon Street, one block over. It's wild after dark. You'd love it." I stopped at an art gallery to admire a painting of a swamp scene.

"Then we should go." He stood behind me, resting his hands on my shoulders.

I gazed at his reflection in the glass. "I'm not sure you could control yourself. It's chaotic enough at night."

He slid his arms around me, hugging me from behind, and whispered, "I already promised to be a good demon."

His breath against my ear made me shiver. "Okay. But just for a few minutes, and then we go back to the hotel."

"Where I can be a bad demon?" He flicked out his tongue to lick my earlobe.

Hecate have mercy, my knees nearly buckled. I turned to face him. "Only for me."

He drew an X over his heart. "I swear on the throne of Hades."

"I thought Lucifer was king."

"He has many names." He took my hand and guided me toward a side street. Quaint little houses in pastel shades lined the sides of the empty road, and a streetlight cast a hazy glow over a giant pothole.

Chaos tightened his grip on my hand and yanked me behind him. "Don't move."

"What's wrong?" I started forward, but he put his arm out to block me.

"Shadow magic. A group of witches are battling an orc."

"What? Right here around all these houses?" I gripped his arm and followed his gaze to the supposed scene. I saw nothing but a quiet street. "Let's turn around so they can do their thing. We're not supposed to engage here."

"Indeed, I can," he said to the invisible witches. At least, I assumed it was them because I still saw and heard nothing.

"Allow me to be of assistance." Chaos strode toward them and lit a fireball in his hand.

Crappity crap. What part of *fire and water don't mix* did he not understand? The New Orleans covens despised Salem. They swore their city was the magical epicenter of North America, even though Salem had the first witches and the thinnest veil.

I had no idea what they said in response to his display, but he tossed the fireball onto what I assume was the dead orc. The flames blazed and dissipated in seconds. A moment later, the shadow magic rolled away, and I could finally see.

A woman stood with her arms crossed, eyeing Chaos suspiciously, and a wet spot lay on the concrete where Chaos had tossed his fire. Oh jeez. Of course he had to do that in front of a water witch. Way to stay off their radar.

"You." She pointed at me. "Come here."

I held in a groan and walked toward them. "Sorry for the intrusion." I clutched Chaos's arm. "My boyfriend is overly helpful sometimes. We'll be on our way."

She widened her stance, and the three men who were with her fanned out around us. "You saw through our shadow and can summon fire. You're not going anywhere but our coven headquarters. The High Priestess will decide what we do with you."

"That's really not necessary." I squeezed Chaos's arm, reminding him of his promise to be a good demon. "We're just here for a little vacay. If we're not welcome, we'll leave first thing in the morning."

"How did the orc get here if there's no rift?" Chaos asked.

The woman tilted her head, studying him. "We sealed it yesterday. This was the last monster who got through." She cast her gaze to me. "Fire witches who know about the rifts. You must be from Salem."

"No." I shook my head adamantly. "We're from Maine, actually. We're solitary."

She put her hands on her hips. "First an earth witch infiltrated our library, and now we have fire witches in our midst. If Salem wants war, that's what we'll give them."

Shit. Chrys was here. This was bad. So very bad. "Hey, honey?" I squeezed Chaos's arm again. "Remember that promise you made?"

His energy shifted, his magic rising to the surface. "Indeed."

"It's okay if you want to break it."

"Understood." He didn't move, didn't give any indication that he was doing anything at all, but the water witch's eyes widened, and her hands clenched into fists. She looked at us, confusion creasing her brow, and she whirled to face one of the men.

"What are you doing?" she screeched.

The man stiffened. "What are *you* doing."

One man shoved the other, and I tugged on Chaos's arm. "Time to go."

We turned and pounded pavement back to Royal Street before making a sharp right and heading for the hotel. Inside, I cast a ward to shroud our magic and hoped to Hecate they didn't see which way we ran.

"Chrys believed the book was with the coven." He sat on the edge of the bed. "Why?"

I shook my head and paced the small room. "She must have used magic to search. A location spell might show her the general area, but it wouldn't be precise." I stopped and dropped down next to him.

"She has Mayhem's skull. I bet she used it as a conduit to scry for his mark. Good gravy, she's a strong witch."

"Not as strong as you." He grasped my hand. "Why did you not scry for it?"

"Because searching for it the mundane way was faster and didn't use any vim. If she figures out it's in the public library, we're screwed."

"Then will have to get to it before she does."

I sighed hard. It looked like breaking and entering was on my to-do list after all.

# CHAPTER 6
# CHAOS

Donned in all black, Ash had tied her hair into a knot on top of her head and pulled a knit cap over it, concealing her blue locks. With her bag of spells slung over her shoulder, she crept down the road, her gaze bouncing this way and that, her muscles tensing more than I'd ever seen them before.

I walked beside her, resting my hand on her back and wishing I could send her a pulse of magic through my mark to calm her. But I'd made a promise never to use magic on her without permission, and I would uphold it. I would do anything for her.

"I understand that you're saving your vim, but the amount of stress you're feeling right now will deplete your energy as well."

"It's fine. We're almost there." A light indicated we

could cross the six-lane thoroughfare, and Ash jogged to the opposite side. I followed, and after another block and then a right turn, the library came into view.

The multistory building had darkened windows, save for one on the bottom floor near the front entrance. Ash looked at it, scrunched her nose in an adorable way, and paced past the doors and around the side.

Stopping at a service entrance, she took my hand and pulled me into the shadows. "There's probably a security guard in there. If he catches us, can you handle him without hurting him?"

"I will do my best."

She tugged her lock-picking kit from her bag. "I'm serious. Just scramble his mind long enough for us to grab the book and make sure he doesn't remember what we look like."

Interesting. She'd gone from *don't use your magic under any circumstance* to my power being her first line of defense. "I can't guarantee he won't destroy any books. I know you are particular about libraries."

Her shoulders dropped with her hard exhale. "You're right. Change of plans. We find the guard first. I'll cast a binding spell, and we'll haul ass upstairs, grab the book and get out before he knows what hit him."

"That is an excellent plan."

She slid two pieces of metal into the lock and moved them around until it clicked. The handle moved down when she pressed it, but the door didn't budge. "Dammit. It's deadbolted from the inside. I'll have to use magic to unlock it."

"Might there be an alarm system?"

"Might you have mentioned that concern before I tried to open the door?" She straightened and adjusted the knit cap on her head. "If there is one, the keypad to turn it off isn't going to be here. There must be another door the employees enter through. Come on."

We crept along the back of the library and turned up the left side. Another door with a light above it stood near the front corner. "Will you be able to disarm the alarm without the code?"

Her mouth screwed to one side as she took out her lock-picking tools. "I think so. If not, we'll have to run. We've already put ourselves on the coven's radar. We can't risk getting into trouble with the law too."

The law didn't worry me in the slightest. Ash might not approve of the ways I could handle them, but she didn't need to worry about the police. I was about to tell her as much when she opened the door, and an incessant beeping sounded in the entry.

She grabbed my arm, pulled me inside, and shined her phone's light onto the wall. A panel with illumi-nated numbers screeched, and Ash held her hands over it, whispering a spell. It beeped three more times in quick succession before glorious silence filled the room.

"Whew. I am so glad that worked." She paced across the room and pressed her back against the wall before peeking through the doorway. Waving her hand, she told me to move aside, so I joined her against the wall.

"What's your plan?" I asked in a hushed voice.

"The security guard is coming this way." She clutched a potion bottle in her hand and removed the cork. "Standing tall or on your knees, in the name of the goddess, I force you to freeze." She tossed the potion at the guard, and he immediately stilled, his eyelids the only part of him that could move.

"How long will your spell last?" I asked as I followed her down the hall and toward a staircase.

"My vim is stronger since we got rid of Chrys's hex on our house, so ten to fifteen minutes. Let's grab the book and jet."

I couldn't help but smile as we ascended the stairs and Ash made a sharp left toward a doorway. "You know where to find the book. Your newfound power has grown exponentially."

"It's so weird." She plucked a thick volume from the shelf and laid it on a table. "I hardly have to try anymore."

She opened the book to the index and ran her

finger down the page before tapping it and flipping through. "Thank the goddess this book is legit. Do those look right to you?"

She turned the book toward me and pointed to the entries about my brothers and me. Multiple paragraphs described our physical appearance and our place in the hierarchy. How in Hell's name did humans know so much about us?

"The sigils do look correct."

She pointed to Mayhem's mark. "I told you it curved left."

"Hmm. I stand corrected."

She took her phone from her pocket and snapped a photo of the page.

"I thought we were removing the book from public access."

"We are, but I'm not taking any chances. I'm texting the picture to Ember now, so we'll be ready when we get his skull. I don't want to lug this giant book around everywhere we go." She closed it and put it in her bag.

"Very smart."

"I tend to be." She winked, making my chest heat, and nodded toward the stairs.

We made our way down and past the security guard who still stood frozen in the hall. He blinked but otherwise seemed incoherent of what happened around him.

"That is a handy spell," I said as we exited the building.

"Sure is."

Ash closed the door and stayed close to the wall, slinking toward the back of the building. "We'll take this to the room, and I'll see if I can get us an earlier flight tomorrow. The sooner we can get out of New Orleans, the better."

"Leaving so soon? But the party just started." Chrys stepped out from the shadows and rested her hands on her hips.

Ash gasped, stopping in her tracks and stepping backward into me. I clutched her shoulders and moved her aside so I could block whatever magic Chrys might throw at her.

"Hand it over, Ash. Don't make this difficult." She clutched a knife in one hand.

"You have no idea what you're dealing with." Ash stepped forward. "If you summon Mayhem, the veil will be torn to shreds and Salem will be overrun with beasts. Surely you don't want to destroy the entire town."

Chrys scoffed. "Says the woman who already summoned Chaos. I'd hoped he'd plow through my hex on Patrice's house. Vanquishing him then would have saved me a lot of trouble, but this actually worked out in my favor."

"How so?" Ash slipped her hand into her bag.

"You led me right to the book I needed. Scrying only gets you so far, as I'm sure you know. Now, give it to me."

"You'll have to kill me first." Ash took a bottle from her satchel, but before she could activate it, Chrys threw her knife. The blade sliced into her hand, knocking the potion to the ground, where it shattered, rendering the spell useless.

Talons protruded from my fingertips as fury ignited an inferno in my soul. My horns extended from my skull, and as my muscles coiled, preparing me to lunge, a gunshot exploded from behind me and pain ripped through my shoulder.

I roared and whirled around to see the culprit: the security guard, who now trembled in his boots. With a grunt, I scrambled his mind. He turned and ran, his head slamming into the brick wall with such force, his skull cracked and caved inward. Blood poured from the gash on his forehead as he thudded on the pavement, dead.

Ash used the distraction to her advantage, running and tackling Chrys. She groaned as her back hit the ground, and Ash pinned her shoulders, holding them down with her knees. "Why are you doing this?"

Chrys struggled beneath her weight. "I need the demon."

"Chaos, can you hold her?" Ash shouted.

I rotated my shoulder and stormed toward them.

Chrys groaned again, and a root from a nearby magnolia tree snaked around Ash's waist, jerking her to the ground. The earth witch yanked the bag from Ash's shoulder and scrambled to her feet, shouting in Latin and raising her hand toward me. A pulse of dark magic slammed into my chest, making me stumble back.

I pushed forward, and another pulse hit my head, then my injured shoulder. The next pulse stopped me in my tracks. Magic wavered in front of me, a wall that could have been made of steel.

"Stop right there, demon." Chrys curled her other hand into a fist, and the roots tightened around Ash. The ground rumbled, the pavement splitting open like a fissure, revealing the earth below. "Or I will bury her so deep no one will ever find her body."

Ash struggled against the roots, grunting as she strained, while Chrys poured a circle of salt, speaking in Latin again. I slammed my shoulder against the spell and broke through, rushing to my witch's side. Gripping the roots, I pulled, trying to free her, but the harder I pulled the tighter they became.

She wheezed, shaking her head. "Any tighter and I can't breathe."

I rose and faced Chrys. "Release her."

The spell complete, she dusted off her hands. "Or what?"

I called on my chaos magic, sending it toward her

and trying to scramble her brain. It had no effect. She had figured out a way to block me. "I'll kill you," I growled.

"No, you won't. Earth magic doesn't die with the caster. Those roots are very much alive, and if I stop controlling them, they'll return to the ground...taking Ash with them."

"It's true," Ash said. "Just like my fire would continue to burn."

"If you want to save your girlfriend, step into the circle." Chrys gestured to the containment ring she'd drawn on the ground.

"Don't do it," Ash ground out. "She'll vanquish you, and I'll die anyway."

Surprise flashed across Chrys's face. "The sigil connects you? I assume that works both ways then?"

Ash pressed her lips together, refusing to speak.

"We can always find out." She flicked her wrist, and a root snaked around Ash's neck. "If you die, and he gets vanquished, I can easily summon him back now that I have the sigils. What will it be, lover boy? I'm about to snap her neck, so make up your mind."

I looked from Ash to Chrys. "Will you release her if I comply?"

"Of course." She waved a hand flippantly. "You have my word."

"Chaos, no! She's lying."

My stomach soured as I watched the root tighten

around her neck. Chrys wanted to command me, to force me to do her bidding, and Ash's life was her currency. Stepping into her circle gave Ash her only chance at survival. "Agreed."

"Please." Ash struggled, her adrenaline causing her fingertips to spark, and a tiny flame danced across a root, charring the surface. It seemed our adversary hadn't bothered to make her trap fireproof.

"Allow me to say goodbye." I took a tentative step toward my witch. When the roots didn't tighten, I continued, kicking dirt over the small amount of smoke rising from the burned area. Kneeling beside her, I pressed a kiss to her forehead. "Everyone underestimates you, but your fire will continue to burn."

"Don't," she whispered.

Chrys laughed. "Ash's fire. That's funny."

Her dismissal confirmed my suspicion. I stepped into the circle. "Let your fire burn."

# CHAPTER 7
# ASH

Let my fire burn? Was he serious? Surely he didn't just offer himself up to a dark witch, thinking I could burn my way out of this mess, because I had already tried. All I'd managed was a miniature flame that barely singed the root, and then he'd kicked dirt over it.

Wait... My little spark had burned the root. She didn't bother with a fireproofing spell because, as Chaos said, she underestimated me. Everyone underestimated me, and that was his plan. For me to somehow tap into my dysfunctional fire magic, burn my way out of this trap, and defeat an earth witch whose power was stronger than anyone I'd ever seen...even Cinder.

Riiiight... I should have gone to Hell with Chaos when I had the chance.

Chrys popped the top off a potion bottle and recited Shade's spell, "Hide from sight our magical plight. With the power of Shade, my intent is conveyed."

Shadows rolled around us, casting the rest of the world in grayscale. If she'd done that from the beginning, maybe the security guard would have survived. Not that she cared about the lives of others, but I did. And my body count was adding up.

She crossed her arms, screwing her mouth to one side. "This is a conundrum. I'd planned to force you into submission and kill Ash. Now, I'll have to keep her alive in order to use you."

Chaos growled. "Ash has claimed me. No spell you could cast will change that. I belong to her and her alone."

She cocked her head. "Careful, demon, or I'll send you back to prison with your brother."

"You don't have the power." He curled his hands into fists, his talons and horns retreating, returning him to his full human form, and I couldn't begin to fathom why.

Well, I guess I could. He was counting on me to save the day for some goddess-knew-why reason, but he was stronger in his demon form. Why on earth would he limit himself?

"You don't have a clue. None of you do." Chrys

took a grimoire from her bag and opened it to a book-marked page.

I wiggled beneath the roots, trying to free my arm. If I'd thought to strap a dagger to my thigh, I might be able to cut my way out of this, but no. I'd hyper-focused on getting that damn encyclopedia and didn't consider that Chrys might follow us. That we might lead her right to it.

"Why are you doing this?" I asked for the umpteenth time. "Cinder was your best friend. Our coven, our family, has been nothing but good to you. We treated you like a sister."

"Quit your whining." She snapped the book shut and returned it to her bag. "Cinder betrayed me, Ember's ego is more than I can bare, and you screw up everything you touch. Salem will be a better place without the three of you."

She snapped her fingers, and the roots tightened around me, the dirt beneath me rumbling, turning to quicksand. "I'll be calling on you again soon," she said to Chaos before turning on her heel and darting into the night, no doubt heading back to Salem to enact her plan.

And here we were again. Chrys had decided to kill me after all, and why not? With the sigils and Mayhem's skull in her possession, she could summon him and Chaos in one circle. Hell, she could probably drag Discord away from Cinder if she wanted to. It would have been the perfect time to say *I told you so* if I wasn't in the process of being buried alive.

Chaos slammed his shoulder against the circle's magic, letting out a roar when it didn't shatter. Maybe if he set his inner demon free, he'd have a chance, but no. He stayed in his human form. "Burn through, Ash. You can do it."

Dirt piled up around me as I sank farther and farther into the earth. My pulse sprinted, my chest squeezing like a vice until I could barely breathe. Did I ever mention being buried alive was at the top of my phobias list?

Burn through. How could I do that when a tiny spark was all I could ever manage? "I can't."

"You can." He punched the invisible wall, and the magic shimmered. "Search your soul. It's deep inside you, ready to come out. Use the adrenaline in your veins, and light those roots ablaze."

"Thanks for the pep talk." The roots pulled me deeper. Dirt covered my legs. If I waited much longer, whatever fire I could summon wouldn't have the oxygen it needed to burn.

I took a deep breath and focused on my inborn power. Either nothing would happen, or I'd turn New Orleans into an inferno. I'd have to chance it.

"Goddess, please help me." I drew magic from the core of my being, raising it to the surface. My veins heated, and sparks formed on my fingertips.

"You can do it, Ash." Chaos slammed against the circle again. "I know you can."

I had to, and I could. At least I thought I could. I had to think I could, or it wouldn't work. I was like the Little Engine. *I think I can. I think I can.*

Curling my fingers toward my palms, I gathered my fire, igniting a ball in each hand. I let the fire roll down onto the roots, but the dirt shifted, dousing the flame before it could do any damage.

A fist of dread clenched in my stomach. That was all the fire I'd ever been capable of summoning, and with my legs covered in dirt, it was useless. "There's no way."

I sank deeper, deeper. My grave covered my hips and hands.

"There is a way." He pressed his palms to the ring of magic containing him. "Remember when I was inside you. The fire ignited on your arms as we fought the fae."

"That was you." I wiggled some more, making my dire situation worse.

"No, Ash. That was your fire. I accessed it, but it belonged to you."

Yeah, right. "I can't do that. Believe me, it was all you."

"So you're going to let Chrys destroy your coven? She'll murder your sisters and turn your town dark, and you're going to lie there and take it like an impotent runt?" He lit his hands on fire and bashed them against the circle. The magic shimmered but didn't wane.

Anger sparked in my chest, battling my fear for control. "I'm *not* an impotent runt."

"No?" His talons extended, and he jabbed them against the magic, making it pulse. "Are you sure? Because that's exactly how you're acting. Like a useless, spoiled runt."

My teeth clenched tightly until a sharp pain shot through my jaw. Where did he get off calling me a runt when he was trapped in a containment circle? A circle he *voluntarily* walked into, even though I told him she'd kill me anyway.

Fury billowed in my chest, making my blood boil and my fire magic rise to the surface.

Chaos's hands returned to normal, and he held them up in surrender. "Go ahead then. Let Chrys win. Let her murder your coven for you. You'd have done it yourself eventually."

My rage surged, coursing through my veins. "I would *never* hurt my family."

"How many people have already died in your wake?" He crossed his arms. "How many more will?"

"I haven't killed anyone!" I strained. Every muscle in my body tensed. Fire churned in my gut and rolled down my arms, gathering in my hands and turning them hotter than a crematorium. Hotter than they'd ever been before.

Flames exploded from my palms, sending dirt flying through the air.

Magical fire rushed up my arms, circling my chest and turning Chrys's roots to soot. I screamed and slammed my flaming arms onto my legs, incinerating the rest of my organic chains before scrambling out of my grave. Thank the goddess I wore fireproof clothes.

My body still ablaze, I marched toward the circle, my nostrils flaring as I clenched my hands into fists. "Don't you ever call me a runt again. I'm an effing Holland witch."

Chaos smiled, nodding his head like a proud papa. "The shadow magic is retreating. I suggest you douse your flames before someone sees you."

"I..." My standard answer of *I can't* nearly crossed my lips, but I looked at the fire dancing on my arms and sucked in a trembling breath. I'd done it. I'd burned my way out of Chrys's death trap and lit half my body ablaze. Even Ember couldn't do that.

"Take a deep breath." Chaos demonstrated as if I didn't know how to breathe.

I did as he said, inhaling as deeply as I could and letting it out slowly. When nothing happened, I did it again.

"Focus on the core of your being, where your magic resides. Do you feel the source of the flames?"

I concentrated and searched, finding the cradle of my magic directly below my breastbone. Resting my hand on the spot, I took another breath.

"Call it back inside. Don't try to force it. Just allow it to return home."

Relaxing my body, I closed my eyes and centered myself, imagining the source opening and allowing the fire to return.

"You're straining. Relax your jaw."

I parted my teeth and took another deep, cleansing breath. The fire rolled back inside me, gathering in my chest and calming to embers. Holy crap.

A laugh blurted from my throat. "That was insane."

"That was your magic."

I shook my finger at my demon. "I've got a good mind to leave you in the circle, mister. What you said was cruel."

He shrugged. "I said what I had to say to force you into acting."

"It wasn't nice."

"I wasn't trying to be."

I kicked my boot through the salt ring, freeing him, and tugged my phone from my back pocket. Whew. It was still intact. If I'd set my whole body on fire, it would have melted and we'd have been screwed.

"Let's get back to the hotel. We'll head for the

airport first thing in the morning and try to get on an earlier flight." I texted Ember, telling her to be on the lookout for Chrys.

"You aren't worried Chrys will summon Mayhem tonight?"

"She won't do it here. Taking over Salem is her goal, so she'll want to have him there. She thinks I'm dead, which would mean you're vanquished. It would be a helluva lot easier to control you both if she didn't have to transport you fifteen hundred miles." I led the way out of the back alley, and we crossed Canal Street before heading into the French Quarter.

"She has a head start and the sigils. She could make it to Salem and summon my brother long before we return if we wait."

Crappity crap. He was right. After everything that just went down, my mind was reeling. I couldn't think straight. But I'd set my arms on fire! "We'll grab our stuff and head there now."

Chaos took my hand. "I hope you know I didn't mean a word of what I said back there."

I waited for a horse-drawn carriage to pass the intersection before darting across the street. "Didn't you though?"

He held his thumb close to his pointer finger. "Maybe about your behavior, but I have never believed you're useless."

"I know, and apparently, I needed to hear it.

Though it freaks me out to think it took absolute fury for me to unleash it. That's not a good quality in a light witch."

His brow furrowed, but he didn't offer an answer. I didn't have one either, and we didn't have time to ponder it. Maybe after we saved the world, I could try to figure it out.

We made it to the hotel without incident—thank the goddess—and grabbed our bags. Well, I grabbed my bag of clothes. Chrys had, once again, taken my satchel full of spells. At least she didn't destroy it this time.

Then again, she now had an arsenal at her disposal. Not that she needed the help. She'd managed to arm herself against Chaos's brain-scrambling magic and nearly killed me. Twice.

I cast a longing look at the comfy, king-sized bed and allowed myself a moment of regret for not letting Chaos be a bad demon when I'd had the chance.

He wrapped his arms around me and brushed his lips to mine. "We will have another opportunity to play."

"Will we?" I rested my head on his shoulder. "Seems like everything will be nonstop from here."

"Everyone has to sleep at some point, and I will make certain you're relaxed enough to slumber when that time arrives."

The feel of his strong arms wrapped around me

and the warmth of his embrace made me ache all over. I wanted him more than I'd ever wanted anyone in my life, and not just in a playtime kind of way. He complemented me in a way I never dreamed anyone could.

Yeah, he'd royally pissed me off back at the library, but it was exactly what I'd needed to save us both. He always knew what I needed.

Chaos made me a better witch. A better woman.

I swallowed the lump in my throat and pulled from his embrace. "We should go. I don't have the ingredients to cloak us on the way to the airport, and I'm certain the local coven we ticked off is looking for us."

I swiped open the Uber app and called for a ride. "Should be here in five. Let's head down."

Outside the hotel, a cast-iron table with two chairs stood beneath a magnolia tree. How nice it would have been to enjoy a nightcap in the warm fall air before going inside and letting this Prince of Hell bang my brains out.

We passed the table and stepped outside the fence to wait for our ride. A group of women wearing hot pink sashes walked by, two of them helping the one with a white veil remain on her feet. Across the street, a man with a scraggly beard sat against the building, balancing a cardboard sign against his legs as he dozed off.

Both New Orleans and Salem were tourist destinations teeming with magic, yet the atmosphere, the vibe, couldn't have been more different. A fist of regret tightened in my chest because I would never get to explore the magic and wonder of this city with the man by my side.

Oof. I had to stop thinking about the end. Regret was another one of those useless emotions Chaos mentioned. It did absolutely no good, so I needed to make like Elsa and let it go. We'd be home in Salem before I knew it, battling a dark witch for a demon skull and literally breaking Hell loose.

Goddess, help us all.

I checked my phone. The Uber sat in traffic a block away. I was about to suggest we go to it when a fog rolled over us, casting the world into grayscale.

"Shit." My heart hammered in my chest, and I clutched Chaos's arm, dragging him toward the car. "Is it Chrys?"

"You tell me." His gaze darted around the shadow spell's perimeter.

Right. I could locate people close by as easily as objects now. With a deep inhale, I focused on Chrys's energy, searching the area for her vibration. "I don't sense her."

The Uber stood four yards away. Just a few more steps...

My muscles seized mid-stride. A heaviness pressed down on me, squeezing, making me completely immobile. I cut my gaze to Chaos. He was frozen too. The Uber turned the corner, heading toward the hotel, and I tried to shout. My voice didn't work. My vision tunneled. The only sound I heard was my pulse whooshing in my ears.

Then silence.

# CHAPTER 8
# ASH

My brain throbbed in my skull, and I pressed the heels of my hands to my temples, countering the pressure. I opened my eyes to bright white light, and my stomach lurched. Sitting up, I dry heaved, thanking the goddess my dinner didn't splatter on the floor.

"Ash?" The familiar voice calmed me, and I looked up to find Chaos standing behind a set of iron bars.

I blinked and rubbed my eyes, trying to focus. "Where are we?"

"Are you okay?" He started to grab the bars but fisted his hands, dropping them to his sides instead.

"I think so. What happened?" My vision returned to normal, and the pounding in my head lessened to a dull ache.

He exhaled, some of the tension releasing from his

shoulders. "We're imprisoned in a coven house. The cells neutralize magic, even mine, and the bars are enchanted with some sort of pain spell. I don't advise touching them."

"Sounds like you know that from experience." I stood and took in my surroundings. My cell had three wooden walls and an iron gate. A cot sat on the hardwood in the middle of the small space, and an unnecessarily bright light fixture hung from a beam above.

Chaos stood across the hall in an identical enclosure, his jaw tight, a vein protruding from his forehead. "Only an elemental witch would be powerful enough to contain me for this long."

"Yeah, the New Orleans covens are run by water witches." I turned to the back wall and lifted a hand to knock my fist against it.

"Don't."

The moment my knuckles met the wood, an electric jolt zipped up my arm and exploded through my body like a million needles jabbing me from the inside out. "Son of a bitch!"

I clutched my chest, making sure my heart still beat. The sensation felt a lot like the electrification spell in Boston.

"The walls are enchanted as well," Chaos said.

"No kidding." I opened and closed my fist, the pain slowly subsiding as I rolled my neck. "I don't remember anything after the shadow rolled over us. Do you?"

"I was mildly coherent through it all. Though my vision blurred too much for me to identify the culprits, their voices sounded like the ones we encountered yesterday."

"Yesterday?" I snapped my gaze to his eyes. "We've been here all night?"

"When I leaned against the bars, I saw the door at the end of the hall. I assume daylight illuminated the edges, though it could have been a yellow electric light."

"Crap. Crappity, crap, crap, crap. Chrys must be in Salem by now. Has she summoned Mayhem? Can you sense him?"

"I sense nothing outside these walls."

"We need to warn my sister." I slapped my back pocket. Of course they'd taken my phone. "Ugh! What are we going to do? Chrys could be using Mayhem to destroy everything as we speak. We have to get you home. You're the only one who can stop him."

His lips twitched. "They have not only electrified the bars and neutralized our magic, but they have also cast a containment circle around each cell. I'm afraid we're at their mercy until they arrive to retrieve us. They want to question us."

"Of course they do. We're fire witches who know about the rifts." I sank onto the cot and pinched the bridge of my nose. "Okay, let's get our story straight. I had no idea the rifts were spreading, and they'll surely blame us. Who knows what Chrys told them."

He crossed his arms. "My chaos magic normally works through any containment or suppression spell. Unless they know what I am and have guarded themselves against my power, I will be able to drive them mad. If you'll allow me, I can make it so they don't remember we were ever here."

"And then what?" I dropped my hands into my lap. "Unless you can control their minds and make them let us out, we'll still be stuck in here."

He frowned. "No, my magic is about disorder, not control. I cannot command anyone in a maddened state."

"They'd end up killing each other, and we'd be left to rot."

He arched a brow. "Unless one of the witches who dies is the one whose magic has trapped us."

I laughed dryly. That Chaos. He always looked on the bright side of destruction, didn't he? "As tempting as that sounds, I think our best bet is to tell them what's going on. We can blame it all on Chrys, tell them she's summoning the demons, and we have to go to Salem to stop her."

He pressed his lips together, nodding as he considered my plan. "And you believe they'll simply let us go?"

"If we're convincing enough, why wouldn't they?"

He clasped his hands behind his back. "You are forgetting that New Orleans contains both light and dark covens, and we don't know which one has imprisoned us."

"Then I guess we'll have to play it by ear."

"If they're dark witches, my plan will—"

"We'll play it by ear."

We would have to because the door at the end of the hall swung open and sunlight flooded the corridor. I cocked my head, giving Chaos a look that I hoped to Hecate said *let me handle this*. He opened his hands, palms toward me, conceding control...at least for the moment.

"Here they are," a woman's voice drifted down the hall, and three or four sets of footsteps followed. It was hard to make out just how people planned to interrogate us until they came into view.

The brunette water witch we saw yesterday evening, two of the men who'd accompanied her, a big beefy guy I'd never seen, and a tall, lanky blonde, who had to be their High Priestess, made five. Damn. This was serious, and I couldn't tell if they were dark, light, or something in-between, thanks to the hex they'd placed on these cells.

And how the hell did they remember who we were? Chaos must've been holding back when he fried their brains.

"They claimed they were from Maine," our elemental friend said. "But their IDs show Salem addresses." She handed the little plastic cards to the High Priestess.

"Thank you, Sandra." She looked at our IDs, her brows lifting as she read mine. "And this one is a Holland witch." She strolled toward me. "A member of Salem's founding family, causing trouble and telling lies in our city. Explain yourself."

"We didn't come here to cause trouble." I started to reach for the bars, but I remembered what had happened when I touched the wall and thought better of it.

The Priestess handed our IDs to Sandra and crossed her arms. "Then tell me, Ash, why are you and Shade here?"

I flicked my gaze to Chaos. I'd forgotten about the glamour on Shade's license. Thank the goddess it hadn't worn off. "Just a little vaycay."

She tilted her head like a disapproving mother. "That's not what your earth witch told us when we caught her in our library."

I crossed my arms to mimic her posture. "Whatever she told you was a lie."

"Says the witch who's been lying since she got here." A man with curly black hair stepped forward. "How can you see through my magic? I'm a master shadow caster. No one can penetrate my spells."

The High Priestess put her hand against his chest, pushing him back. "Calm down, Umbra. They're elementals. They have power you can't imagine."

He narrowed his eyes. "Elementals aren't all that."

Oh, for Hecate's sake. Was it a requirement that all shadow witches had egos for days? "I can't see through your magic. Shade can because it's one of his inborn powers. I don't know how he does it."

Chaos shrugged, acting cool as an icicle. "I have always been able to see through shadow."

"Nobody has that much power," Umbra said.

"He obviously does." The Priestess gave him a pointed look, and he backpedaled to join the other four.

"Look." I raised my hands in surrender. "It's true we aren't here on vacation. We lied because we didn't want to stir up any trouble, but we obviously made it worse by not being upfront. We aren't the enemy."

"The earth witch you found in your library is the true adversary," Chaos said. "She is the reason the veil is weakening, and she plans to destroy it when she returns to Salem."

"Funny." She rested a hand on her hip, shifting her weight to her right leg. "That's the same story she told us about you."

My hands instinctively curled into fists. "She has an encyclopedia of demons. She's planning to summon a Prince of Hell, and if we don't get back to

Salem soon, she'll do it. You think the rifts are bad now? Wait and see what happens if you don't let us go."

She looked me up and down. "Your friend told me about your curse." She held a hand toward my chest and inhaled deeply, calling on an inborn power, I assumed. "It's as I suspected. Someone...your mother, maybe...blocked your fire magic. She did everything she could to stop you from fulfilling your destiny, but destiny...fate...can't be avoided. You will be responsible for your coven's demise one way or another."

I tried to keep a neutral expression, but damn. My mom blocked my magic? All these years, I'd thought I was defective, when my power had been bound all along. What the actual eff, Mom?

"You didn't know." She pressed her lips together, looking at me with pity. "It doesn't matter. I won't let you summon more demons. We've already had to join forces with the other covens to fight off the monsters coming through. It ends now."

"It's Chrys you want," I said. "She has the book. She's going to summon the demon."

The High Priestess turned, flipping her hair over her shoulder and lifting a hand as she walked away. "Kill them."

That answered my question. We'd landed ourselves in a dark coven's prison.

"Fast or slow?" Umbra cracked his knuckles and stood in front of my cell.

A wicked smile curved Sandra's lips. "Slow deaths are always sweeter."

"Works for me." He shoved his hand into his pocket and pulled out a handful of one-inch-long capsules in red, purple, blue, and green. With a chuckle, he touched each one, no doubt trying to decide which spell he wanted to throw at me first.

He closed his fist around them and searched his pocket for another one, and I had to admit packaging spells like that would be convenient. They took up a helluva lot less space than the bottles I used, but the thing I was most envious of was his pocket size. He could hold fifty spells in each one, with how deep they went. If my pants even had pockets, I'd be lucky if they were three inches. Maybe I should start wearing guys' clothes if I made it out of this in one piece.

"Here we go." He held a black capsule between his thumb and forefinger.

"Don't use that one." Sandra held her hands in front of her chest, gathering the moisture from the air between her palms and creating a ball of water. "I want her to watch her boyfriend die."

Chaos crossed his arms, looking bored. Unless Sandra could sharpen that ball into a sword and stab him through the heart, she would be sorely disappointed.

Umbra's jaw tightened. "If she's blinded, she can only hear his screams. That'll be even better."

She whirled to face him. "She watches. Put your shadow away."

His nostrils flared as he blew out a breath, but he returned the black capsule to his pocket and decided on the purple one. Without even whispering a spell, he wound his arm back and threw it like a baseball. I half-expected it to bounce off the hex surrounding the cell, or at least to fizzle out upon impact. Instead, it sailed right between the bars and exploded against my stomach, and let me tell you, that little pill felt more like a cinder block slamming into my gut.

I careened backward, my shoulders slamming against the electrified wall, sending a jolt rocketing through my body. Fabulous. Their magic could get in, but I couldn't even summon mine, much less throw it at them.

I stretched my neck and shook off the pain. "I didn't know New Orleans witches were such cowards. Why don't you let us out so it can be a fair fight?"

Umbra glared at me and reached toward the lock.

"Don't," one of the henchmen finally got the courage to speak. "They'll burn us alive."

Sandra sent a blast of water with the force of a firehose at Chaos's chest. I was sure she meant to knock him back into the wall like Umbra had just done to me, but my demon held his ground. Her magic soaked his shirt but didn't hurt him in the least.

He laughed. "Is that the best you can do?"

"I'm just getting started." She hurled a stream of water at him, but he stepped out of the way. It splashed against the back wall, the electricity spell zapping the liquid and turning it into steam.

"Javon, freeze them both." Sandra stepped back, letting a henchman approach Chaos's cell. Umbra handed him two green capsules, and Javon cast a binding spell on my demon.

Honestly, I couldn't tell if the hex worked on him or not. He didn't move a muscle, so he was either pretending so he didn't reveal his true identity or it did work and we were screwed.

Javon pinched the capsule and threw it at me before reciting the binding spell. On me, it definitely worked. Starting at my feet, my muscles seized. I tried to wiggle my toes inside my boots, but I'd lost control. The magic crept upward, freezing my legs, my abdomen, my neck. I was a fish in a barrel, and Umbra was about to cock his gun.

Sandra shot another stream at Chaos. It hit his arm and sliced open the skin, but he didn't reward her with a reaction. She hit the other arm and then his shoulder, ripping his shirt. He still looked bored AF, even with blood dripping down his arms.

"Give me a nerve spell." She held her hand toward

Umbra, and he placed a red capsule in her palm. "Let's see if you stay stoic with this one."

Oh, dear. Unless they knew of some secret ingredient for that one, he most definitely would stay stoic. Nerve spells didn't affect the Princes of Hell. Not this prince, anyway.

She cast it, and Chaos closed his eyes, his face pinching. Again, he could have been faking. "I expected dark witches to practice more unsavory magic. Especially an elemental. Has someone bound your power too?"

Holy crap, he could talk. "Way to blow your cover." I clamped my mouth shut. I could talk too. And my mind worked perfectly. If we got out of this mess, I'd have to swipe those capsules to see if I could reverse engineer their binding spell.

"Cover?" Sandra faced Chaos. "What is she talking about."

He inclined his chin, refusing to speak.

She turned toward me, her eyes calculating. "Change of plans. He's going to watch her die. Hit her with everything you've got."

"Gladly." Umber gathered shadows between his palms that looked way too much like Shade's when he'd summoned his magic to kill the rose bush.

I willed my legs to move, to let me step back, away from the icky, sticky funk of dark magic, but they didn't budge. He sent the shadow toward me, and it rolled around my body, encasing me in agony as it dimmed my inner light, sucking the life out of me.

"Chaos," I wheezed, hoping that was enough to let him know he could use whatever magic he needed to get us out of this place.

Umbra's eyes widened, and he blinked three times. His magic released me, the shadows rolling back into him. I heaved two heavy breaths. If I hadn't been frozen, I might have collapsed to the floor. Ouch.

"Umbra!" Sandra shouted. "What are you doing?"

He spun around. "I'm done taking orders from you."

"The hell you are." She shoved him into the bars, zapping him like a mosquito in a bug trap.

He roared and barreled toward her, knocking her into Chaos's bars. She screamed and peeled herself away. Javon threw a punch at the other henchman, clipping him in the jaw. He fought back, and the four of them brawled like they were in a bar fight.

Chaos had bought us some time, but without the use of my magic, I couldn't unlock these doors. He couldn't bust through them, thanks to the containment circle, so we were still stuck. *Think, Ash. Think.*

I looked down, my head finally able to move. The binding spell was wearing off slowly, but these witches would kill each other before I could come up with a plan. Maybe, if the one who cast the spells to keep us in died in this fight, we'd be able to get out like Chaos said. But I had a feeling the High Priestess herself set up this prison. Only someone with immense power could deny an elemental access to her inborn gifts.

My shoulders moved, and I gazed at my arm. My sleeve covered Chaos's mark, but it heated in response to his magic. I wondered...

"Do you think our bond works both ways?"

He walked toward the bars. "What do you mean?"

Sandra sent a wave of water toward Umbra, knocking him off his feet. Javon kicked him while he was down, landing a boot in his stomach. The other guy kicked his head.

"I'm going to try sending my power to you. Hopefully my magic will counter yours, and you'll have control of their minds." It sounded logical, anyway. He was madness; I was order. It was worth a shot.

He raised his brows. "That might just work."

My fingers moved. Then my wrists. Finally my arms were free. Lifting my sleeve, I ran my hand over the mark. Chaos let out a slow exhale. One day I'd remember to ask him what that felt like.

I centered myself, taking three deep breaths and focusing on my connection to my demon. I couldn't summon magic from the core of my being inside this cell, so instead, I thought about Chaos. I imagined the way my body reacted when he sent his power into me. The way it calmed me and helped my mind focus.

"Do you feel anything?" I rubbed the sigil again.

His gaze locked with mine, his expression going from concentration to wonder. He turned his head toward the fray and said, "Order."

The witches stopped fighting, Javon in mid-swing, and turned toward Chaos. Umbra groaned in a pool of blood on the floor.

"Release us," Chaos said.

"I..." Sandra's brow furrowed in confusion.

"Open the gates and let us go," my demon commanded.

"Yeah." She held her hands over the lock and recited a spell. The door swung open, breaking the ring of salt, and Chaos stepped out of his cell.

"Now her." He gestured to me, and Sandra shuffled to my side before casting the same unlocking spell.

I hauled ass out of there and clutched Chaos's arm. "Ask her for our IDs."

He held out his hand, and Sandra dropped the licenses into his palm. "Our bags," he said.

"They're in the main house."

I took the IDs and shoved them into my back pocket. "Can you make it so they don't remember any of this?"

"Not while I'm channeling you."

"Okay. I'll let you go." I pulled down my sleeve, and drew my energy inward, breaking the connection.

"Come on." I tugged him toward the exit while Sandra and her gang turned on each other once more.

We stepped into the daylight, and I squinted against the brightness. A massive stone fountain bubbled in the center of a cobblestone courtyard, and decorative troughs lined the perimeter, with water pouring from stone heads mounted to the walls. Muffled shouts echoed from the carriage house where we'd spent the night, but the rest of the air hung soundless, still. Someone had cast a silencing spell over the entire property, allowing nothing out or in.

"Forget about our bags, let's find a cab and get to the airport." I clutched his hand and made my way toward a gate. "Don't let them kill each other."

"The moment we step off the property, I will release them."

"You're not going anywhere." The High Priestess appeared from the main house and lifted a hand toward the fountain. A tidal wave blasted toward us.

# CHAPTER 9
# CHAOS

I shot a line of hellfire onto the ground and raised my hands. The flames surged, creating a barrier to counter the witch's magic. My fire consumed her wave, turning it to steam the moment it met the flames.

"Impressive." She crossed her arms. "I collect elementals, you know. Perhaps you'd like to stay." Her gaze flicked to our right, where another witch hid in the shadows.

A single root ruptured from the earth and snaked toward Ash before looping around her ankle.

"Hecate on a Hellhound, this is getting old." Ash shook her leg and then bent down yanking the root free. Another one shot upward to her wrist, but she easily removed that one as well. The Priestess might have collected elementals, but her earth witch was either very young or very weak.

Another root snaked toward Ash, and she stomped her boot on it, pinning it to the dirt. "Listen, you do not want to see me use my fire magic right now, because I will burn your entire coven house to the ground and it won't even be on purpose."

I held in a laugh, certain she meant that she would lose control of whatever fire she created. In reality, she could raze this entire city if she could summon the fury to counter the block her mother put on her power.

"So Salem does want war. We can accommodate that." The Priestess pointed at Ash and turned her hand over, curling her fingers one by one toward her palm.

Ash gasped, and sweat beaded on her forehead before gushing from her pores. Tears rained from her eyes, and each exhale released a puff of steam.

I called my wall of fire back to me and stepped between them, blocking her magic from reaching my witch.

"She was dehydrating me." Ash sucked in a giant breath. "I need water." She lunged for the fountain, scooping the water into her hands and sucking down as much as she could.

The Priestess pointed at me before making the

same motion with her fingers. "I'm the most powerful elemental on this continent. No witch can defeat me."

This time, I didn't hold in my laugh. "No, you are not, and I am not a witch."

I unleashed my chaos magic in full force, sending it outward to cover the entire property. A panicked scream ripped from the Priestess's throat, and the earth witch stepped out from the shadows, clawing at her face and making it bleed.

Ash tried to stand, but she stumbled, falling backward onto the cobblestone. With our adversaries going insane, I scooped her from the ground, bent her over my shoulder, and carried her through the gate.

"Turn it off." She tapped my back. "It's affecting me too."

I took a deep breath and drew my magic inward. The force with which I had hit them would render them incapable of remembering the past four hours. Possibly the past twenty-four. When we reached the end of the block, I lowered Ash to her feet, holding her tightly until she regained her bearings.

"Will they survive?" She clutched my biceps and swayed.

I pulled her to my chest. "Their minds will recover, though they'll have no memories of the events. I have no way of knowing what they did to each other while I held them."

She nodded and wrapped her arms around my waist. "I need water. Maybe a hospital."

Her skin felt dry, and as I brushed my thumb across her face, it flaked. "You need a healer."

"Well, Patrice is a thousand miles away, so..." Her pallor turned ashen.

"You said there is a light coven here. We'll find it and ask—"

"No." She pulled back, squinting her eyes against the sunlight. "No more witches. I just need a bag of IV fluids, and I'll be fine."

"IV fluids? What are they? Where can I get them?"

"A hospital, but that would take too long. I bet there's an IV bar or three around here somewhere." She turned and took a single step before swaying on her feet and clutching her head. "I can't. I can't walk; I'm too woozy."

"I will carry you." I made to pick her up as I had carried her before, but she shook her head.

"That'll draw too much attention. I'll have to ride piggyback." She motioned for me to turn around, so I obeyed. With her hands on my shoulders, she lifted one leg toward my hip. "Pull me up."

I helped her onto my back, and we ventured deeper into the city.

"Hang a right here. Once we get closer to Bourbon Street, we can ask for directions."

Music grew louder as we approached, and the

sidewalks filled with people. The sun hung high in the cloudless sky, illuminating the smiles of the humans walking by.

"Excuse me," Ash said to a woman in a black t-shirt with the name of a bar embroidered on the breast. "Can you point me toward an IV bar?"

Sympathy creased the woman's brow. "Rough night, huh?"

"You have no idea."

"Two blocks that way, on the right." She pointed down the street. "They swear they've got a forty-five-minute hangover cure. Thankfully, I've never had to try it."

"Sounds like exactly what I need. Thank you."

"Anytime." The woman continued on her way, and I walked in the direction she had pointed.

"Oh, crap." Ash tightened her grip on my shoulders. "I don't have a way to pay. My wallet was in the satchel Chrys took."

I continued my trek. "Yet the ID cards and phone were in your pocket. Why not carry everything of importance on your person?"

Her laugh turned into a cough. "Have you seen girl pockets?"

"Apparently not."

"I put the IDs in my back pocket because a lot of places here want to see them before they'll let you inside. My phone went in the other one, and nothing would fit in my front pockets, especially in these pants. They're two inches deep."

"What's the point of adding them to clothing if they'll be of no use?"

"Right? There it is." She pointed to the next building. A sign that read *The Original Forty-Five Minute Hangover Cure* hung above a blue door. She groaned. "I have to stop talking. My throat is so dry."

"Then stop talking."

"But we still don't have a way to pay."

"We won't need to pay."

"These are innocent humans. You can't scramble their brains. Maybe I can get some free water at a fast-food restaurant."

"You can't even walk, Ash. If this will make you better, you'll have it." I opened the door and stepped inside before she could argue. "My girlfriend requires hydration."

"It's fine. I really don't think—"

"Is payment required in advance?" I asked the man behind the counter.

He stood and motioned me toward a reclined chair. "You can pay on your way out. Have a seat."

I situated Ash in the chair, and he handed her a plastic card. "Have a look at the menu, and I'll get a tech for you."

He walked into a back room, and Ash glared at me.

"You can't keep hurting people. That's not how this works."

"If you are hydrated, will your magic function properly?"

"Yeah. I haven't used any vim today, but—"

"When it's time to pay, connect with me the way you did in the prison. We will simply convince them that we don't need to pay."

She opened her mouth to argue but paused and closed her lips.

I took her hand. "It's for the greater good. You are the only one who can defeat Chrys, and I am the only one who can reason with Mayhem. We must make you well so we can return to Salem."

"Fine. Just this once but give me the cheapest one." She handed the menu to me, and I scanned the offerings.

A woman wearing a beige shirt and pants smiled as she approached. "Hi, I'm Ashley. What can I do for you?"

"She'll have the deluxe hydration and vitamin package." I gave the menu to her before Ash could see that I requested the most expensive option they offered.

"Perfect. Let's get you hooked up." She took Ash's left arm and pushed up her sleeve. "That's a beautiful tattoo."

Ash's eyes widened in alarm, but when the tech

didn't say more, she relaxed. "Thanks."

The woman rubbed alcohol on Ash's skin at the bend of her elbow before sticking her with a thick needle. Ash winced, and the woman removed the needle, leaving a piece of plastic tubing in its place. "It takes about forty-five minutes to complete. Can I get you some water while you wait?"

"Yes, thank you."

"You got it." She opened a small refrigerator and offered some to us both. "Are you going next?"

"No, I feel fine." I accepted mine and twisted off the cap.

She nodded and returned to the back room as Ash drank her entire bottle.

I took a sip and brushed a strand of hair from her face. "Is your full name Ashley like hers?"

"Nope. Mom stayed true to the fire theme when she named us. I asked her why we didn't have normal names once. She said it was because we aren't normal women." She shrugged and leaned her head back, closing her eyes.

"She was right about that." I watched her rest, the color returning to her cheeks as the fluids replenished her system, the anger I felt toward the High Priestess for doing this to her growing with each passing second.

I couldn't begin to imagine the pain Ash must have felt. If I hadn't intervened, she would have died an agonizing death, and for that, the dark witch would pay. I could make good on Ash's threat to burn their entire coven house to the ground, including every witch inside.

The fluids would take another half hour to replenish her. I could kill them all and be back before it was done.

"Don't even think about it." Ash opened her eyes, pinning me with a familiar look. "You're staying right here."

I relaxed the tension from my shoulders. She knew me too well. "She deserves to suffer."

"No. Bad demon." She fought a smile.

"How could you tell what I was planning?" I took her hand in mine.

"Your energy changes when you get mad and start plotting. Plus, the tendons in your neck get so tight I could pluck them like guitar strings."

"I see."

"When this is done, we're getting on the plane, and we are never coming to New Orleans again."

"It's a shame. I rather like this city, aside from the infuriating witches hellbent on destroying you." I sat back in my chair, and we watched a program on the television while the fluids dripped into Ash's arm.

When the bag emptied, the tech removed the tubing and wrapped a pink bandage around her elbow. "How do you feel?"

"Much better, thank you." Ash stood and took two tentative steps forward.

"You can check out at the front desk. Have a great day." The tech smiled warmly and gestured us toward the man behind the counter.

We approached, and I looked at Ash, waiting for her to create the connection. She ran her finger down my mark, and I shivered as the sensation of her caressing every inch of my skin at once washed over me. A moment later, her magic flowed into me, and I activated mine, sending it to the man at the desk. He snapped his gaze to me and blinked twice, awaiting my command.

"The treatment was complimentary," I said. "We'll be leaving now."

He looked at Ash and then at me. "Yeah, of course. Don't forget to give us a good review on Yelp."

"I will. Thanks." Ash took a business card from the desk before walking out the door.

I met her on the sidewalk and took her hand. "We make a good team."

She shook her head. "We can never do that again. Mind control isn't the light witch way."

"How do you plan to travel to the airport then? I'm afraid it's too far to walk."

"Crap." She waved at a yellow car. "Okay. We'll do it one more time."

# CHAPTER 10

# ASH

"You're joking." Ember paced the length of the kitchen. "Tell me you're joking."

"I wish I was." I sat at the counter next to Chaos and took a sip of beer. Patrice had gone shopping again, and our fridge was now fully stocked. She'd also emptied the dishwasher and swept the floors while we were gone. Maybe we could keep her around...

"You had one job. Go to New Orleans, get the book, and come home." Ember stopped and rested her hands on the counter. "And I specifically told you not to interact with the witches there."

I rolled my eyes. "It's not like we went looking for trouble."

"You don't have to. Trouble follows him everywhere he goes." She grabbed a beer from the fridge and popped the top before taking a long pull. "Mind control, Ash? That's not just bad. That's goddess-smiting-you bad."

"It was for the greater good, so I think I'll be okay." I hoped I would anyway. Besides, even the goddess had a few shades of gray in her.

She sighed, her shoulders drooping with her exhale. "Don't do it again."

"I don't plan to."

Chaos downed his beer and set the empty bottle on the counter. "Neither do I. I much prefer causing pandemonium."

I laughed. "See? Problem solved. Now, where is everyone?"

"Patrice is with Miles and Shade, working on a fae infestation. We try to keep at least one person at home to protect the house, so here I am." She hoisted herself onto the counter and swung her legs. "I'm glad you got a picture of the sigils, but Chrys has the book and the skull. I'm surprised she hasn't summoned Mayhem yet."

"I will feel it when she does." Chaos stood and carried his bottle to the recycle bin. "But if we can find her first and summon him ourselves, he will be easier to control."

"And that's easier said than done," Ember said. "She's shrouded herself like she did to Shade. We tried scrying for her this morning and found nothing. Not even an inkling of where she might be."

"Did you visit her home and place of employment?" he asked.

She laughed dryly. "And every other place in Salem she frequents. She hasn't been to her job in more than a week. I tracked down her mom's phone number and called her. She said Chrys stopped talking to her years ago. There's no telling where she's hiding."

"I can scry with you," I said. "Chaos helped us find Shade, so I'm sure he can cut through her spell and help."

"I couldn't cast a spell to save my life tonight." She typed something on her phone and stood. "We battled three beasties and sealed two rifts this morning, in addition to the scrying. I'm spent, and the others will be too when they get back. We need to recharge."

"Can you scry alone, or does it require two witches?" Chaos asked.

I nodded. "Chaos and I can give it a try."

My sister crossed her arms. "Don't bother. I just tried it alone half an hour before you got here, and even if you did find her, we're all too weak to fight tonight. Tomorrow, she could be somewhere else. Save your vim, unless Chaos senses Mayhem."

We both looked at him, and he shook his head. "Nothing yet."

"I found out something else while we were in New

Orleans." I drummed my fingers on the counter, hesitating to ask my question. If her answer was yes, I wasn't sure how I'd feel, but I had to know. "Were you aware that Mom bound my fire magic to keep me from fulfilling the curse?"

Her eyes widened, and she blinked in surprise. "No. Who told you that?"

"The High Priestess had some kind of inborn power to detect magic. She said I was blocked."

She wrinkled her nose like she'd whiffed a foul fart. "And you believe her? She's a dark witch. They lie."

I picked at the label on my half-drunk bottle. "Chrys didn't just tie me up and take my bag. She left me to die. Her roots were trying to bury me alive, and I burned my way out of it. For once in my life, my fire magic worked the way it's supposed to."

"You." She paced the kitchen again. "Why didn't you lead with this? How? What happened?"

"Chaos pissed me off so much, my fury got around the block." I couldn't fight my smile. "Ember, I set my *arms* on fire. My whole upper body. I burned through the roots, and when I got out, I called the fire back inside."

"She was incredible." Chaos stood behind me and squeezed my shoulders.

Ember's mouth hung open. "Holy crap, sis."

"Chrys underestimated Ash and didn't bother with fireproofing." He grabbed another beer from the fridge and tipped it back. "She assumes Ash can only do spell work, which is why she keeps taking her bags. We can use this to our advantage. Ash can be our secret weapon."

"If we can figure out how to remove this block." I took a swig of beer and grimaced. It was already room temperature, so I pushed it away.

He took my bottle and dumped the contents into the sink before dropping it in the bin. What a good demon he was turning out to be. "You can call on your power around the magical block."

"Only if I'm royally pissed off."

"If Chrys doesn't do it for you, I'm sure I can." He winked, making my stomach flutter.

"No." Ember shook her head. "It's too risky. I won't take a chance that big. You have to figure out how to remove it."

I rested my elbow on the counter, cradling my chin in my hand. "It's on my miles-long to-do list."

"Move it to the top." She crossed her arms. "As in figure it out tonight. If Mom bound your magic, it must be in a grimoire in our library somewhere. Find it. Figure out how to reverse it. Tomorrow, we'll find Chrys and put an end to this shitshow."

She made it sound so simple. "You're not the slightest bit worried I'll screw up—this time epically because I'm at full power—and burn the entire town to the ground?"

She lifted one shoulder dismissively. "Not in the slightest."

"And you shouldn't be either." Chaos opened the door, waiting for me to get up.

I slid off my stool and shuffled toward him. "Excuse me for not having as much faith in myself as you do. I've been defective my entire life."

Ember threw her arms into the air. "Oh, for Hecate's sake, Ash. Get over yourself. You're a badass, you always have been, and if you can reverse Mom's spell, you'll be the baddest ass of us all. I'm going to bed. The others should be here in an hour. Yell if there's a problem you can't handle." She started toward the hall but stopped. "No one else needs to know about this. If you're going to be our secret weapon, we need to keep you a secret. Don't tell the others. Not even Patrice."

My bottom lip had started to poke out, so I drew it in as she walked away. "Okay. I guess we're looking for a spell book." I headed down the stairs.

Chaos followed. "Your sister is correct. I've told you from the beginning you're the most powerful witch I've ever seen. Your inborn location ability, your mastery of ink, and now your fire powers being unlocked... Few witches are blessed with so many gifts."

"Maybe." I stopped at my desk and rested my hands on the back of the chair. "Maybe you're right, but it took me summoning a Prince of Hell into my head to realize any of it."

He squeezed my shoulders. "Of course that's what it took. You were meant to summon me. Fate brought us together, Ash. You can't deny it."

I sighed and turned to face him. No, I couldn't deny it any longer. The way we fit together, the way we worked together, our powers contrasting and complementing each other... If fate wasn't to blame for this messy, effed-up relationship between a light witch and a demon, I didn't know what was. We were perfect together. Too perfect for it to have happened any other way.

"I can admit that now. You and I were supposed to happen, and I won't pretend we weren't. The problem is, when I find the spell my mom used to bind my magic, if I can reverse it, that's it. No more Ash the screw-up. No more excuses for staying in my little library alone."

He put his hands on my hips, and I rested mine against his chest. "And that's a bad thing?" he asked.

"Yes. I mean, no but yes at the same time. It's become a sort of crutch. When everyone's expectations of you are low to nil, you never let anyone down. Without any limitations, I..."

"You can grow into the witch you are meant to be. Think of the possibilities."

"I am, that's why I'm scared." I tucked my hair behind my ear. "What if we fail? What if I unlock my magic, we go after Chrys, but we still fail?"

"You won't fail."

"But what if we do? With my magic bound, we could blame it on Ash the screw-up." I tugged on my bottom lip before worrying it between my teeth.

"Why would you want to hold on to that? You're too smart, too kind, and far too powerful to be the coven's scapegoat. It's time you came into your own, and I am looking forward to sharing the experience with you."

"Ugh." I tipped my head back to look at the ceiling. "It's just been this way for so long, I don't know how to be anything else."

"You're a fast learner. You'll figure it out quickly."

I looked into his eyes, a sense of resolve washing over me. "You're right. It's time I stopped hiding behind my weaknesses. I'm an effing Holland witch, and I need to act like one. I deserve respect."

"You should demand it." He shook his fist, rallying me even more.

"I should. I'm going to find that book and reverse this spell, and then Chrys isn't going to know what hit her. I'll be the Stealth Bomber. A ninja. A Jack-in-the-box that pops before it's supposed to and scares the crap out of anyone who plays with it." I marched toward the stacks.

"That's my girl. Silent but deadly."

I stopped short and spun around. "That's what my dad calls his farts, and I am not a puff of stinky wind."

"You are a hurricane."

"Damn right I am." I had to think. Binding magic was used way back when during the witch hunts to keep children from revealing their powers. Mothers would bind their magic when they were out in public and release it when they made it to the safety of home. I'd bet my left boob that's what my mom did to me.

"It'll be an old book, circa the sixteen hundreds."

"Don't think too hard. Let your magic guide you." He picked up a stack of books from the floor and set them on a shelf.

The excitement of my little speech had my heart racing, so I took a deep, cleansing breath and centered myself. "What spell did you use to bind me and where is the book?"

A tug in my chest led me to the back of the library, straight to the secret shelf where we'd found the aura-shrouding spell. A pale yellow book with a cloth cover leaned haphazardly against the end of the unit, and I grabbed it, flipping it open to the correct page.

My mother's elegant handwriting filled the margin. "'Spell must be rejuvenated every six months to keep fire subdued.'"

A lump formed in my throat, and I swallowed hard. "She's been casting the spell on me every six months for my entire life, and I didn't have a clue."

He rested his hand on my lower back and peered at the page. "How long have your parents been missing?"

"About six months." I carried the book to my desk and laid it open.

"That would explain why you could tap into your full power in New Orleans. The binding is losing its potency, and your fury helped you break through."

"Huh." Pressure built in the back of my eyes, and a sob threatened to escape my throat. "This is such a simple spell. I mean, I guess it had to be for parents to be able to cast it every day without depleting their vim. She just..."

Another sob rolled up from my chest, and I swallowed it too. "I know she did it for the greater good, but damn. Couldn't she have told me what was going on? If I'd known why my magic didn't work right... Did she not realize what it did to my self-esteem?"

He pulled me to his chest. "I'm sure she did what she thought was best."

Tears gathered on my lower lids. I blinked them away and pulled from his embrace. "It doesn't matter. I can break the spell. It's so effing simple." I scoffed at the ludicrousness of it all. My entire sense of self-worth had been determined by a spell used on kindergarteners in the sixteen hundreds. Sadly, that tracked for old Ash.

Not anymore.

"Let's go to the kitchen. I'll need a potion." I carried the book upstairs and set it on the counter before gathering my copper bowl and my mortar and pestle. Eucalyptus, hyssop, and sage combined with lemon oil would dissolve whatever was left of the binding, and I could...

"You're still afraid." Chaos's deep voice drew me from my thoughts.

I blinked and stared at the counter where I'd laid out everything I needed for the potion but hadn't mixed a thing. "Not scared, no. It's surreal to think about. If we had time to wait, my magic would come back on its own. I don't know. This is weird."

"Indeed." He opened two herb jars and slid them toward me. "But if you want to finish this before the others arrive, you should get started."

I crushed the eucalyptus and hyssop and mixed it with the powdered sage before adding three drops of lemon oil. It flashed and sizzled, and I dumped it into a half-glass of water and swirled it around. "Undo, unbind the magic I find. Set me free. So mote it be."

The liquid turned pale blue, and my heart hammered in my chest, excitement making my hands tremble. I took a deep breath, and then another, while Chaos watched me intently.

"Bottoms up." I pressed the cool glass to my lips and tipped it back, downing the contents in two gulps. My stomach burned and bubbled, a fizzy sensation rising to my chest before cascading down my arms and legs. A fist clenched in the core of my being, and an audible *pop* sounded from deep within, flooding my veins with heat.

I set the glass in the sink and looked at my hands. Was that it? Could my magic flow freely like it was supposed to now?

Chaos raised a brow. "And...?"

It felt rather anticlimactic for the thing that killed my self-esteem and made me feel like a failure my entire life to break that easily, but it was a simple spell. Simple, yet so effing powerful it had shaped the woman I had become.

And now...I was free.

I focused on my inborn power, feeling it churn in my chest before it surged down my arms. My fingers sparked, and I curled them inward, igniting a fireball in each palm. I held them up, even with my eyes, and watched the flames blaze.

"Call it inward," Chaos said.

Normally, if I summoned fire into my hands, I had to send it somewhere—into a sigil to activate it, the sink to extinguish it, the dry leaves in the cemetery to burn the place to the ground. This time, I focused on the source of the flames in the center of my being and opened it, allowing the fire to return to the place from which it came.

I closed my fists, and the fire just...went away like it was supposed to.

Sending the sparks back to my fingertips, I created two new fireballs in my palms. I closed my fists again, and it returned inside me.

A laugh rolled up from my chest, and I did it again, and a fourth time. "Do you see this?"

Chaos smiled. "Indeed, I do. Can you send the flames up your arms?"

I opened my hands, creating the fire, and focused on sending it upward. My arms ignited like Ember's sword, the flames licking up to my shoulders, my head spinning with giddy excitement. "Holy Hecate! Do you think I could do my whole body?"

"Are your clothes fireproof?"

My heart sank, and I extinguished the inferno. "No, dammit." I'd changed into my comfies when we got back home from New Orleans.

"Oh, I know what I can try. Ember can send out fire, and if it hits the wrong thing, it'll bounce back without charring anything." I rubbed my hands together and locked my gaze on the backsplash above the sink. Gathering a fireball in my right hand, I thought about my intent and hurled it, calling it back the moment it hit its target.

Only, it didn't come back.

The ball exploded, and flames licked up the back-splash, toward the window, setting the curtains ablaze.

"Crap!" I rushed to the sink, ready to douse it with water.

"Call it back," Chaos said. "You don't need water."

I looked at the faucet in my hand and the flames turning the curtains to smoke. "Yeah, okay." Focusing on the source, I opened up, allowing the flames to return inside me. The fire extinguished almost instantly, but not before it set off the smoke alarm.

A high-pitched squeal pierced the room, and I grabbed a dishtowel to wave in front of the offending device. Ember rushed into the kitchen, just as Patrice and the guys walked through the door.

"What the hell?" My sister raked a hand through her hair.

"Sorry. I uh..." I cut my gaze toward Miles and Shade. "It was an accident."

Shade shook his head and walked by without a word, and Miles followed. Patrice flashed a sympathetic look toward me before asking Chaos, "Still no Mayhem?"

"She has not summoned him yet."

"Good. I need some sleep." She shuffled through the living room and disappeared down the hall.

When everyone was out of earshot, Ember asked, "It didn't work?"

I flashed a ginormous smile and nodded.

"It did?"

"Yes!" I did a little excited jump and giggled. "No more blocks."

She cut her gaze to the charred curtains before giving me a look.

"She will need practice." Chaos wrapped an arm around my waist, tugging me to his side. "Her power is unique. It will take time for her to learn the nuances of what she can do."

"That's amazing." She yawned. "But don't practice out here. Those three don't have the best poker faces, and I want Chrys to underestimate you as much as possible."

I saluted her, my smile so big, my cheeks ached.

"Go to bed. We need to be operating at full capacity to take down Chrys." She turned and walked away.

"I'm too excited to go to sleep." I bounced on my toes.

Chaos laughed. "Come on, little witch. Let's get you to bed."

# CHAPTER II
# ASH

"I hate this." I sat on the edge of my bed and wrung my hands. "I'm not tired at all, Chrys has to be somewhere in Salem, and I feel like we should be looking for her."

Chaos sat next to me and stilled my hands. "I agree. How long will it take the others to recharge now that Chrys's hex has been broken?"

"A few hours, minimum."

"And if you scried for her, how long would you need to recover?"

I turned my head to meet his gaze. "It depends on how long it takes and how much of your energy I use, but you're not suggesting we go after her on our own, are you?"

He lifted his hands, palms up. "Your team is in no condition to fight, but you and I—"

I shook my head. "Let me stop you right there. She has bested us twice already and nearly killed us both times. When we face her, it needs to be all six of us."

"But your fire..."

"Is supposed to be a secret. If we go after her now, and she gets away again, we lose the element of surprise. She thinks I'm dead. Let her keep thinking that." I stood and turned down the bed. His plan was tempting. I couldn't deny that, but we had to be logical about this, and logic was my jam.

"Just because this magic inside me has been unlocked, it doesn't change who I am. Ash Holland always has a plan. She's cautious and rational. She doesn't run off on tirades just because she can. Ember's the adrenaline junkie. I'm the librarian, and that's not going to change. I'm not going to abandon everything I stand for and join the leap-first-look-later crew. I'm always going to look, and I'm going to make damn certain the people I love do too."

He grinned, his gaze dancing over my face as he rose to his feet. "You are absolutely right. You are the librarian, the Ink Master, the logical, rational witch who has, against the laws of nature, found a home inside the heart of Chaos."

I crossed my arms, trying to ignore the warmth spreading through my chest at his words.

"You have kept your sister in check through all of this, your spells saving her life on multiple occasions.

Can you see, now, how powerful you are? How powerful you have always been?" He rested his hands on my hips, pinning me with his emerald gaze. "Can you see yourself the way I see you?"

I laughed and clasped my fingers behind his neck. "My entire life, I've been *just*. Just a librarian. Just an apprentice. Just a screwup. Just...Ash." My chest tightened, not in a fist of dread, but of intense gratitude. "But I'm not *just* Ash."

"No, you are not."

"I'm Ash effing Holland, and I have you to thank for making me realize that."

He slid his arms behind my back, tugging me closer until our hips met. "I told you we were meant to be."

"And this couldn't have happened any other way." I rose onto my toes and pressed a kiss to my demon's lips. *My* demon. He planned to lift my curse, but he had already saved me.

An *mmm* rumbled from his throat, and he slid his hands down to grab my butt, pressing his hips harder against me. As if I couldn't already feel just how happy he was to hear me say that. Lucky for both of us, I had plenty of vim to cast a silencing spell on my room, no potion required.

I stepped out of his embrace, and his expression morphed into that of a predator. His eyes narrowed, his nostrils flaring as he inhaled my scent. "Don't back away from me, little witch."

Heat pooled below my navel, my lady bits throbbing between my legs. I couldn't tell you what it was, but every time he called me his little witch, I felt like I needed to change my panties. He prowled toward me, and I put my hand on his chest, stopping him.

"Two things first," I said. "Do you sense Mayhem in this realm?"

He closed his eyes and took three deep breaths, going utterly still. "No, but even if I did, I'd tell you he could wait."

A thousand butterflies danced in my stomach, flitting up to my chest. "Then give me a second to cast a silencing spell over the room, so I can have my way with you without the whole house hearing it."

He peeled off his shirt and tossed it onto the dresser before dropping his pants to the floor, and boy, oh boy, I almost forgot all about that spell I wanted to cast. Seriously, my gaze locked on his dick, and all thought drained from my brain, letting my hooha call the shots.

He chuckled. "Any day now."

I sucked in a breath, snapping out of my trance. "Right."

After reciting the incantation, I tugged my oversized t-shirt off and tossed it next to his. "Ready to be my bad demon?"

His pupils constricted, the green undulating like a stormy sea. The sigil on my arm heated in reaction to his arousal, and as he stalked toward me, I ran my fingers over the mark. He growled his approval.

"What does that feel like?" I asked.

"Like you are caressing every inch of me all at once. Pleasure in its purest form." He cradled my cheeks in his hands and lowered his mouth to mine. Our lips met, and, faster than I could blink, he swept an arm beneath my knees and carried me to the bed.

His kiss was urgent yet gentle as he lowered me onto the mattress, but when I wrapped my hand around his dick, he groaned into my mouth. I wiggled out of my sweatpants, tossing them aside and pulling him down on top of me.

Spreading my legs, I wrapped them around his waist and reached for his cock. He took it into his hand before I could, and rubbed the head between my folds, teasing me. I groaned and lifted my hips, all but begging him to fill me, and he pulled away, sitting up on his knees.

I rose to meet him and crushed my mouth to his. He held me tightly, wrapping his arms around me and drinking me in. "Take me," I whispered against his lips. "I'm yours."

He broke the kiss, his brow furrowing over passionate eyes. "Do you mean that?"

"Goddess, yes. I need you inside me right now." I reached for his dick, but he grabbed my wrist, stopping me. I tried with the other hand. He gripped that one too, and having both my wrists clutched in his strong grasp turned me on to no end. If I could growl like him, I would have. *Rawr.*

"You said you're mine." He slid off the end of the bed, pulling me toward him as he stood. "Are you mine?"

The intensity of his gaze nearly drew the breath from my lungs. He stepped back, tugging me off the bed until we stood face to face, my wrists still firmly in his grasp. My heart slammed against my ribs, my breaths growing shallow and more rapid as I gazed into his eyes.

Was I his? Could my heart belong to a creature from the Underworld? To a Prince of Hell? I sucked in a sharp breath as the realization sank in, and I swallowed the thickness from my throat. "You and I are meant to be."

"I belong to you, Ash, body and soul. Whether you bear my mark or not, I am yours for eternity, and I will find a way to be with you, whatever the cost." He lowered my arms, finally releasing his grip. "Do you belong to me?"

I rested my hands against his chest. "In every way possible."

He inhaled deeply, holding my gaze, and Ember's words passed through my mind. *What if he falls in love with you? What if you fall in love with him?* It seemed we were about to find out.

"I love you, Chaos."

He slid his fingers into my hair. "And I love you." He held my gaze for another beat or two before leaning in and brushing a gentle kiss to my lips. Pulling away just far enough to see my eyes, he smiled, an incredulous laugh rolling up from his chest. "You are..." He kissed my forehead. "You are everything."

I glided my hand down his stomach, and this time, he let me stroke him. He moaned and leaned his head to mine, trailing his hands over my shoulders, to cup my breasts. With a sudden grunt, he gripped my hips and pulled me toward him. His gaze turned feral, and a deep growl rumbled in his chest, penetrating to my soul.

He grabbed my butt, lifting me from the ground and pinning me against the wall. With one hand, he pulled my thigh up while using the other to guide his length to my slit. In one swift thrust, he filled me, electricity rocketing through my body as I gripped his shoulders and wrapped my legs around his waist.

Leaning into me, he thrust over and over, filling me completely and making every nerve in my body hum. With the wall behind my back and his rock-hard everything pressing into my front, I let out a moan that could have woken the undead in the middle of the day.

He grunted, his fingers gripping my thighs as he pounded his hips. The orgasm coiled in my core, spiraling through my body and releasing like a breaking dam. My nails dug into his shoulders, and I cried out, burying my face into his neck and breathing in his warm, spicy scent.

He thrust one more time, grinding into me and moaning the sexiest moan I had ever heard. Panting, our bodies slick with sweat, he held me there until our breathing slowed. Then, he lowered my legs to the floor and slipped out of me. He kissed my forehead, each cheek, and my mouth before scooping me into his arms and returning me to the bed.

I don't know how long I lay there, silently snuggled in his embrace, but I must've fallen asleep at some point because, when Chaos gasped and shot upright, my heart attempted to escape through my throat. His momentum knocked me off the bed, and I hit the hardwood with a *thwack*, sharp pain shooting through my shoulder, which took the brunt of my fall.

He scrambled to his feet, his eyes wild, every muscle in his body tense. "Mayhem."

I sat up, clutching my aching shoulder. "She summoned him?"

"I think..." He pressed the heels of his hands to his

temples, his gaze bouncing all over the room, not focusing on anything until it landed on me. "Ash."

He raced to my side and kneeled next to me. "What happened? Are you injured?"

"You knocked me out of bed, but I'm okay." Clutching the edge of the mattress, I pulled myself to my feet. "Did Chrys summon your brother?"

"I'm so sorry." He rose and rubbed my shoulder. "Do you need Patrice?"

"I'm fine." I strode to my dresser for some fireproof clothes. Soft morning sunlight streamed in through the window, so snuggle time was over. "What's going on? Were you dreaming, or do you sense Mayhem?"

His brows slammed down over his eyes. "I'm not sure."

I tossed him some clothes. "Get dressed. Whether she summoned him or not, it's time to end this." I winced, a stabbing pain slicing through my heart. Why did I have to choose those words? Ending this meant sending the man I loved to another dimension and never seeing him again.

I couldn't think about that now. Stopping Chrys and saving the coven had to be my first priority.

He shoved his legs into his pants and pulled on a t-shirt. "I sensed him." Closing his eyes, he took three deep breaths. "But I don't anymore."

"Could it have been a dream?" I stepped into the

bathroom and grabbed my hairbrush before raking through my tangled locks. "I've had dreams that were vivid enough to make me swear they were real."

Chaos joined me at the sink and squirted toothpaste on my toothbrush and then his. "It's possible. Or I could have felt him the moment he passed through the veil, and then her shroud concealed him. She is powerful enough to hide his aura from me." He jabbed the toothbrush into his mouth and scrubbed.

We spit and rinsed and made ourselves presentable before heading down the hall to the empty living room. I turned on the lights and strode to the kitchen for breakfast. Chaos stood in the center of the room, confusion tightening his features. If we weren't in crisis mode, I'd have said he looked adorable. But we were counting on his ability to sense his brother.

"Still nothing?" I grabbed a fresh carton of eggs and cracked them into a bowl.

He sucked in a breath. "No. Shall I wake the others?"

"Not yet. Let them recharge fully so we'll be in top shape for whatever's about to go down." I beat the eggs and set a large frying pan on the stove to heat. I couldn't find any bacon in the fridge, but Patrice had bought ham, so I added the thick slices to another pan to heat them up. They popped and sizzled, making the kitchen smell so savory good that my stomach growled.

"Can you start the coffee?" I dumped the scrambled eggs into the pan and stirred them around. "Ten scoops in the filter and a full pot of water."

He smiled softly, a small chuckle emanating from his throat as he poured in the grounds. "This domesticity is quite...quaint. I could get used to it."

"You'd get bored so quickly. Our lives aren't usually this fast-paced."

"I could never be bored with you by my side." He added the water to the machine and turned it on.

Ember strode into the room, dressed in her fighting yoga clothes, and settled onto a stool at the counter. "How's your vim?

"Completely full. You?" I took six plates from the cabinet and set them next to the stove before popping four slices of bread into the toaster.

"Good, because we're all going to need sigils before we go after Chrys." She locked her gaze with mine. "We need protection."

I blinked, my go-to response of *you know I don't do those* threatening to cross my lips. Old Ash would have blurted it out in a nanosecond, but I was new Ash now. "Protection, speed, and strength for everyone. I can do that."

She lifted her brows. "Five sets. You'll be okay?"

"I'm Ash effing Holland. Ink is in my blood." The

coffee maker beeped, so I poured a cup and set it in front of her.

She cut her gaze between Chaos and me. "I like this newfound confidence."

I smiled. "Me too. Soup's on."

We filled our plates, and the others joined us in the kitchen. Coffee, eggs, ham, toast, my demon by my side... I could get used to this domestic life too. Patrice sat next to Ember at the counter, and the rest of us settled at the breakfast table and dug in.

"Do we have a plan?" Miles shoved a forkful of eggs into his mouth.

"Has she summoned Mayhem yet?" Shade asked.

We all looked at Chaos, who flattened his palms on the table. "I'm not sure. I sensed him this morning while I slept, but it only lasted a few seconds. She is either shrouding him, or I dreamed it."

"Did you get a sense of his location when you felt him?" Ember sipped her coffee, watching him over the rim of the mug.

"Sadly, no." Chaos cut a piece of ham and put it in his mouth, chewing and swallowing before he continued. "If she knows anything at all about summoning demons of our level, she will do it in a secluded place, not far from her home."

"We'll have to scry for her." I set my fork on my empty plate and folded my arms on the table.

"We already tried that," Miles said. "We can't cut through her shroud."

"Chaos can." I placed my hand on top of his. Their gazes flicked to where we touched, but nobody bristled at my suggestion. Yay for progress. "He's the reason we found Shade."

"We'll have to do it together," Ember said. "We share the vim so no one gets wiped out."

"So we'll share his magic too?" Patrice bit her lower lip, her forehead creasing.

"It's the only way." I stood and carried my plate to the sink. Chaos joined me, and the others sat silently for half a minute before Shade slapped his hand on the table.

"I'm in." He brought his plate to the sink. "Chrys manipulated me. All of us. I'll do whatever it takes to stop her." He caught my gaze and nodded. "Teamwork."

That was a word I never thought I'd hear Shade utter.

"I'm in too." Miles took the last gulp of his coffee and brought his dishes to the sink as well.

Patrice stacked Ember's plate on top of her own and slid off her stool. "This is crazy. You know that, right?"

"You probably won't even feel him," Ember said. "I didn't know he was helping Ash when we scried for

Shade until I came out of the trance and saw his hand on her shoulder."

Patrice rubbed the back of her neck, her gaze bouncing to each of us before she nodded once. "Okay. Let's do this thing. I'll take care of the dishes while you and Ash set it up."

I grabbed the biggest copper bowl we had and filled it with water. "Here we go…"

# CHAPTER 12
## ASH

Our scrying bowl sat on the floor in the middle of the living room, and the five of us sat cross-legged in a circle around it, so close our knees touched. We'd tried putting everyone at the table, but we couldn't see into the water unless we stood. Sometimes witches passed out during a scrying session, and we couldn't take any chances.

With our luck...*my* luck...someone (me) would fall and smack their head so hard they'd be down for the count. We needed our entire team in top shape if we were going to succeed in our mission. We had twenty-something other coven members and the entire city of Salem counting on us, even though they didn't have a clue what was going on.

Chaos sat behind me, outside of our circle.

Another chance we couldn't take was his magic driving someone mad in the process, so I'd absorb whatever he could give and keep it to myself.

Ember took my left hand, and Shade took my right, which was weird as all get out. I expected him to stay as far away from Chaos and me as possible, but with Patrice still wary of what we were about to do, he'd volunteered to hold my hand just in case Chaos's magic seeped through. Miles and Patrice completed the circle, and we centered ourselves, preparing for the biggest scry of our lives.

I looked each witch in the eyes and started my prayer. "We call on the goddess Hecate to watch over us and keep us safe from harm. Please aid us in finding Chrys and Mayhem so we may right what we've put wrong."

"As we will it, so mote it be," we all said in unison.

We stared into the water, letting our gazes soften. Relaxation washed over me as my vision lost focus, the water turning from clear to inky black. The hardness of the floor beneath me and the warmth of the hands holding mine slipped away, the hum of the furnace and the bustle of tourists outside silencing. The world became still, empty.

I focused on Chrys's energy, picturing her face in the blackness of my trance, searching for signs of her aura.

I felt nothing.

When we scried for Shade, we found him easily. The shroud had kept his location hidden, but his essence still registered in the abyss. With Chrys, it was like scrying for Cinder. Like she'd dropped off the face of the earth.

*"Can anyone sense her?"* Ember asked in our minds.

*"No,"* Miles said. *"Not at all."*

Patrice and Shade confirmed. Chrys was nowhere.

*"Do you think Mayhem took her through the veil?"* I asked.

*"Goddess, I hope not,"* Ember said. *"I'm pulling us out."*

My senses returned, jerking me out of my trance, and I inhaled sharply, opening my eyes and squinting against the living room light. Chaos's hand rested on my shoulder, and I placed mine over his. "It didn't work."

"I felt as much." He pulled his hand away.

I scooted back to sit next to him. "If she summoned him without a containment circle, would he have taken her to Hell?"

His expression darkened. "Without hesitation."

"Well, crap." I extended my legs, letting my boots thud on the floor. "What do we do now?"

"You're sure you don't sense him anywhere in this realm?" Ember grabbed the chair behind her and hauled herself into it. "Could he have killed her?"

Four seconds passed before he replied. "He would

owe her a debt, but if her request was too high..." He clamped his mouth shut and screwed his lips to one side.

One second, two, four, seven. "Demons have a code, a set of rules we follow to keep the balance between worlds. When we are summoned, we can do a mortal's bidding in exchange for a price. Releasing him from prison would be enough compensation for nearly any request, but..."

We all stared at him, waiting for him to continue. When he didn't, I clutched his arm. "But what?"

He let out a slow breath. "Mayhem has never cared much for rules. Lucifer has threatened to exile him on multiple occasions, and, quite frankly, I'm surprised he hasn't yet."

Ember stood, ready to pace, but Chaos and I sat in her path. I tugged him up, and we moved to the couch while the others took the chairs and loveseat.

"You're saying that even though he owed her a debt, he might have killed her anyway?" My sister took up her usual post, passing back and forth in front of the television. "And now he could be roaming free, wreaking havoc all over the place."

"I would sense him if he were in this realm." He clasped my hand.

"So Chrys is gone, and Mayhem is back in Hell." Crappity crap. There'd be no love lost over Chrys getting tortured for all eternity, but we needed Mayhem. We needed them all.

"Great." Shade clapped his hands together. "Problem solved. Send Chaos home, he can send Cinder back, and we're done with the demon infestation."

Ember clenched her jaw. "It's not that simple."

"Why not?" he asked.

"Uh, hello." I raised my hand. "I'll still be cursed to murder the entire coven, and killing me is *not* an option."

He held up his hands in a show of innocence. "I wasn't going to suggest that."

"There's one more possibility." Chaos scooted to the edge of the cushion and rested his elbows on his knees. "Perhaps Chrys simply hasn't summoned him yet. My sensing him before could have been nothing more than a dream."

"But all five of us joined to scry for *her*," Patrice said. "We would have sensed something with that many witches working together."

"Maybe not." Ember dropped into a chair. "Chrys is powerful beyond belief. She knows light and dark magic, and she could be in cahoots with Boston. Maybe five of us couldn't find her because she had help with her shroud."

"It makes sense." Pain etched lines on Miles's forehead. "It's too much of a coincidence for their people to show up here right when Ginger..." He sucked in a shaky breath. "They must be involved."

"She was able to control our guys." Ember shrugged. "Why not Boston witches too?"

I rubbed my forehead and squeezed my eyes shut, willing my brain not to explode. "We need to scry again." I looked at my sister. "We need to look for the skull this time. All six of us."

Shade snapped his head toward me, his lips scrunching like he was about to send me a giant eff you. Instead, he nodded once. "I agree. We can't sit here speculating all day. Let's search for the skull." He lowered to the floor and sat cross-legged in front of the bowl.

"No." Patrice shook her head. "I want to end this as much as you all do, but light witches shouldn't channel demon magic. There has to be another way."

"She's got a point," Miles said. "He's scrambled our brains before. If we invite him in, he might do permanent damage."

"That aspect of my power won't be utilized." Chaos squeezed my hand before sitting across from Shade. "I'll simply heighten the magic you're already using."

I moved to sit next to Chaos. "And I'll take most of it. My magic counters his chaos power. I'm sure I can neutralize it if anything leaks through." I hoped I could at least, because we were out of options. Chrys was hell-bent on destroying our town, and we had to stop her...no bones about it.

Ember sat on the other side of Chaos. "I've channeled him before. It's not that bad." She rubbed her hands on her pants, no doubt remembering the electricity running through her when we set up the ward on the building.

Shade scooted around to my other side. "I've survived his brain scrambling multiple times. I'll chance it."

I gave him the side eye. Where was this sudden sense of comradery coming from? I didn't have a clue, but I wasn't about to question it. We needed to work like a team now more than ever.

Miles plopped down next to Ember and patted the space between him and Shade. "They're right. We're doing it for the greater good. Who's going to defeat the darkness if not us?"

Patrice swallowed hard, her gaze flicking to Ember. She opened her mouth on a big inhale, pausing and holding her breath. I pleaded with my eyes, begging her not to give us all the bird and walk out the door.

She looked at me. "You trust him?"

"With every fiber of my being." I slipped my hand into his.

She glanced at the others, who nodded their encouragement, and she let out a sigh before dropping to the floor. "I trust you, Ash. If you say this is okay, I believe it."

My shoulders slumped with my relief, and I took Ember's hand. "Remember, we're looking for Mayhem's skull. Don't focus on Chrys at all. She won't be far from the skull."

I said another prayer to the goddess, and we all fell into the scrying trance. My senses of sound, smell, and sight slipped into the abyss, taking touch with them, save for Chaos's hand in mine. His skin heated, a slight prickling sensation making my fingers tingle before a surge of energy washed through me.

"*Whoa,*" Ember said in my mind.

I held onto the magic, letting it fill the core of my being as I focused on finding Mayhem's skull. Chrys's stellar shrouding skills kept it hidden, so I slowly let the magic go, sharing Chaos's power with Shade.

"*Holy crap,*" he said as I let it trickle into him.

"*Is everyone okay?*" I asked.

"*It's a rush,*" Miles said.

"*I don't feel any different,*" Patrice said.

"*Shade, let some go.*" Now was not the time for his ego to kick in.

"*Oh,*" Patrice said.

"*Okay. Everyone is channeling, and we're all connected. Let's find the skull.*" I sent out my feelers, picturing a skull in my mind and focusing on the vibrations in the abyss. Chaos sent another pulse of power into me, but I held onto this one, afraid to over-whelm the others.

*"Chaos, do you sense him?"* I asked, but he didn't reply. I searched the nothingness for his essence, but he wasn't in the trance with us. *"Looks like we're on our own."*

We sat silently, searching, feeling, sensing, until Ember drew us toward her. *"There. That has to be it."*

I focused on the space she guided us to, and a low vibration hummed faintly in the darkness. As I drew my consciousness nearer, it intensified until it pene-trated to my bones. *"That's him."*

Chaos's hand tightened around mine, and I searched for him again. I felt Shade, Ember, Miles, and Patrice. Mayhem was unmistakable, but Chaos was nowhere to be found. He must've been reacting to my quickening pulse.

*"Can anyone sense where he is?"* Shade asked.

Another burst of magic surged through me, and this time, I shared it. An image of the skull came to my mind. Then the sensation of coarse fabric against my skin. *"It's in a bag. Do you feel it?"*

*"Is it burlap?"* Miles asked. *"It's scratchy."*

*"It's softer than burlap."* I allowed the sensation to wash over my entire body. *"I think it's wool."*

*"Pull back,"* Ember said. *"It doesn't matter what kind of sack it's in if we can't see where it is."*

I let the coarseness of the fabric go and focused on

the area around the bag. It sat on a slab of thick wood, worn smooth from decades...maybe centuries...of use. A wooden panel stood behind it, and another rose to its right. Was the skull in a bag, inside a box?

*"It's a shelving unit,"* Ember said. *"Where are we?"*

I pulled back further in my mind to take in the scene. A massive antique wood table, a prayer bench, and a four-foot-tall crucifix made the location unmistakable.

*"It's the basement of the big church,"* Miles said. *"I've been there before."*

*"Gotcha,"* Ember said. *"Let's end the session."*

I focused on Chaos's hand holding mind, allowing my physical senses to return. Patrice gasped, and I opened my eyes to find her panting, her hand pressed to her chest.

"Everyone okay?" Ember rubbed her palms together. "No one went crazy?"

"I'm good." Shade released my hand and rubbed his thighs.

"Me too." Miles shuddered and rolled his neck.

"That was...weird." Patrice rose to her feet and paced to the kitchen. "I'm going to make a restorative tea to return our psyches to their normal, nondemonic, states. It should help recharge our vim as well."

"Where is my brother?" Chaos stood, tugging me up with him.

"His skull is in a church basement." I went to the kitchen to help Patrice with the tea. "I guess what you felt this morning was a dream because, unless she made a decoy, his skull is still just a skull."

"It's not a decoy," he said. "I felt his vibration through our bond when you located him."

"Yeah, but you've 'felt' him before." Ember made air quotes. "She fooled you once."

"It won't happen again," Chaos said.

I crushed the herbs Patrice gave to me, and she added them to the metal diffuser before dropping it into a pot of hot water. Holding her hands above the mixture, she recited an incantation, and pink steam rose from the surface. Once it dissipated, she poured the brew into five mugs, and I passed them out.

"Do you need some?" I asked my demon.

He chuckled. "My normal state is fully demonic. I doubt a tea would change that."

I sipped Patrice's potion, and the citrusy flavors of lemongrass and orange zest contrasted the nutty, winter spice blend perfectly. "Does it taste this good without the spell? I could drink this every day."

She smiled. "It does. I'll have to write down the recipe for you."

"Drink up, folks." Ember set her empty mug in the sink. "Then we're heading downstairs for sigils and going after that skull."

# CHAPTER 13

# ASH

"Go to the studio. I need a minute to center myself." I sank into my squeaky chair and waited for the others to leave the library. Everyone filed out except Chaos, but that was fine. I might need a pep talk if I freaked myself out too much.

"You can do this." He massaged my shoulders, easing the tension that had them creeping toward my ears.

"I know." I patted his hand and stood before pacing toward the stacks and grabbing volume four of my sigil collection. I set it on my desk and ran my fingers over the embossed burgundy cover. Familiar magic tingled on my skin, and a sense of calm washed over me.

Real calm, not the fake kind Chaos could force onto me. Sigils were my jam. Ink was in my blood, and even with my fire magic unlocked, I knew *this* was what I was meant to do.

I flipped the book open to the protection symbol and traced the design with my fingertip.

"You aren't familiar with this one?" He tilted his head, examining the page. "Have you done it before?"

"I am, and I have. The last time I drew this one was the day Cinder went missing. I assumed I'd flubbed it, but now I'm not so sure." Because if she went across the veil with Discord willingly...that changed everything.

"What, exactly, does it provide protection against?"

I tapped the sigil. "Hexes, magical attacks, even physical trauma to an extent. It sort of creates a force-field around the bearer."

His brow crept toward his hairline. "It makes you invincible?"

"I wish. Strong magic can still get through, but the sigil helps deflect the weaker stuff. Although, with enough persistence, the weak spells can too. This one wears off quickly with use."

"Your sister summoned a Prince of Hell. Even with the sigil working at full force, he could have easily overcome it."

I closed the book and returned it to the shelf. "Yeah, well, it sounds like she went across the veil with him by choice, so..."

"Another unnecessary hit to your self-esteem has been resolved."

"Exactly. Come on." I led the way into my studio, where Ember had already set up the tattoo machine.

My sister sat first and offered her forearm. I dipped the needle into the enchanted ink and drew the sigils for enhanced strength and speed in record time. Honestly, I probably could've done those two with my eyes closed.

With the first two complete, I added more ink to the needle and pictured the protection sigil in my mind. I drew a circle centered over two perpendicular lines with arrows at each end. A half-moon came next, then a swoosh down on the right side and the left, ending at a fine point.

"That looks absolutely perfect." Ember held up her arm, examining my work. "Next."

My sister got up, and Miles took the seat. He closed his eyes and went into his meditative state like he always did when he got ink. When I finished, I drew the same designs on Shade and Patrice. Then it was time for mine.

Chaos's mark occupied the space on my arm that was easiest to reach, so I had to flip to the opposite side and lay it on the table at an uncomfortable angle to find some free skin. My demon stood in front of me, watching intently, a smile curving his lips.

"What?" I glanced up at him before continuing my tattoos.

"I'm imagining how you must have looked when you drew my mark, so intent on using me to organize your library."

I laughed. "Not nearly this awkward, I promise."

My body tingled as I channeled the magic from the goddess and kept it inside rather than giving it away. The hum of the needle pulsing in and out of my skin filled my ears, and I inhaled deeply against the burning ache. Miles really did need to give a lecture on how to ignore the pain.

With my sigils finished, I let out a slow breath and returned the tattoo machine to its stand. "Ready to light these babies up?"

Shade examined his arm. "You're sure the protection will work? You swore you'd never try them again after Cinder."

Chaos tensed, ready to berate him for questioning my abilities, so I patted his arm. Thankfully, he took the hint because we *had* to operate like a team for this to work.

"Cinder crossed the veil willingly." I returned the ink well to its proper place. "Now that I know what really happened to her, I'm confident in my abilities."

He nodded. "You should be. You do good work."

Wait. What? Did Shade just compliment me? My face scrunched in confusion. "Thanks?"

"You first." Ember held up her finger, so I offered my arm. She shot a tiny, controlled flame onto my sigils, making them glow deep red before fading to cool blue.

My muscles tensed as the magic took hold, my stomach doing flip-flops while my pulse sprinted. Holy Hecate. I wasn't used to having my abilities enhanced. "How much stronger am I?"

I wrapped my arms around Chaos and strained to lift him three inches off the floor. I should have tried a before and after because he still felt heavy as hell.

"Don't waste it." Ember lit Shade's sigils before pointing her finger at Miles. "It lasts about six hours, but the more you use it, the less it works."

I rolled my eyes and laughed. "She says to the Ink Master."

She activated Patrice's sigils, and I clenched my jaw. That was my job. I could do it now. I didn't need the Zippo anymore, and it took all the willpower I could muster to not step in and take over. But Ember was right about their poker faces. We were counting on Chrys underestimating me, so it was best if everyone else did too.

Ember lit the sigils on her arm, and everyone pulled down their sleeves, hiding the protection marks. Chrys wouldn't be expecting those either.

We made our way to the library and gathered our supplies before heading to the back door. Ember grabbed the lever and held up a fist, telling us to wait. She slowly pulled it inward, peeking through the narrow opening, and I bounced on my toes.

These sigils made me feel like I was high on caffeine, and the anticipation of using my newly unlocked fire power had me itching to bust through the door and run to the church. Maybe this was why Ember always seemed so reckless.

No, she was reckless with or without the ink.

I needed to calm the eff down before I forgot who I was and started acting like my sister. I made a mental note to never enhance my speed and strength again and rose onto my toes to whisper in Chaos's ear.

"I can't calm down. Can you help?"

He arched a brow, questioning me, so I pulled up my sleeve and rubbed his mark. With a deep inhale, he closed his eyes, his lips curving upward, and sent a pulse of magic through our bond.

Calmness spread through my veins, warming me from the inside out, slowing my pulse, and relaxing the tension in my legs. I mouthed the words *thank you*, and we followed Ember out the door.

"Were you expecting an ambush?" Chaos asked as we paced toward the van.

"I'm expecting anything and everything she can throw at us." Ember scanned the alley in both directions before climbing into the driver's seat. Patrice took shotgun, and Miles went for the way back seat. I started to get in the back, but Shade cleared his throat.

"Hey, Ash?"

I stopped and turned toward him, and Chaos rested his hand on the small of my back, no doubt ready to defend me against whatever sourness Shade wanted to share.

He opened his mouth and closed it again before nodding. "I'm sorry for the way I've been treating you."

I flinched like he'd slapped me.

He gestured with his head at Chaos. "Does he know about our history?"

"He does…" Wariness lifted my voice.

Shade shrugged. "I don't handle rejection well, and I acted like a dick because of it. And then seeing you two together… I realized I never really got over you and that was fueling it too."

My mouth hung open, whatever words I should have said not even registering in my brain.

"Anyway, with the close calls we've had, I wanted to get that off my chest…just in case."

Chaos climbed into the van, giving us some perceived privacy, and my brain finally started working again. "Umm… Thanks for saying that, Shade. It means a lot, and…"

Now it was my turn to shrug awkwardly. "I'm

sorry too. We've both behaved badly toward each other."

"Cool." He climbed inside without another word, so I did too.

I settled next to Chaos, and he took my hand, lacing our fingers together and giving me a squeeze. Ember started the engine and drove toward the church, where we'd either defeat the enemy and claim the demon or we'd die trying. Some of us might either way.

"Whatever happens, whatever she promises, don't trust her." I patted Chaos's leg. "I mean it. Even if she's got me strung up by the ankles over a pit of vipers, do not believe she'll let me go if you comply."

His jaw tightened, and he glanced at me out of the corner of his eye.

Patrice turned around in her seat. "That sounds like you're speaking from experience."

"We're both lucky to still be in this realm," I said. "When this is over, I'll tell you about it."

Ember's eyes narrowed in the rearview mirror, and she hung a right where she should have gone left. She glared even harder and hung another right before slamming on the brakes. The tires squealed, the van skidding to a stop in the middle of the road. "We're being followed. Arm yourselves."

She hit the gas, and we all turned around to see a

dark brown delivery truck on our tail. "Now, Ash," she shouted.

"Move your feet." I reached down to open the floor compartment and passed out the weapons. Chaos held Ember's sword in his lap, and Miles and Shade strapped on even more knives than they already wore. I attached a dagger to each thigh and offered a sheathed hunting knife to Patrice.

She held up her hands, refusing it. "I don't think I could use that. I'll stick with spells."

"Take it," Ember said. "You might need to cut through some roots."

"Okay." She accepted the knife and strapped it to her right thigh.

Still flooring it, Ember ran through a stop sign and swerved around an old woman driving at granny speed. The woman, with silver hair and decades of wrinkles, gave us the bird, and, if my lip-reading skills were any good, she shouted a string of profanities as we whizzed by.

Our pursuers swerved around her as well, the top-heavy truck lifting onto two wheels for a second before it gently, unnaturally, returned upright. Fabulous. We had a telekinetic on our tails.

I turned to tell Ember what we were dealing with, but the words didn't have time to cross my lips before our wheels locked up and we skidded across the road.

Ember hit the gas, revving the engine, and smoke billowed from the back axle.

"They've got a telekinetic." I opened my satchel and grabbed an undoing potion. I could usually break simple hexes without one, but this magic felt way too strong for just words. "I'll try to counter the spell."

After uncorking the same potion I'd used to unbind my fire magic, I dumped the contents onto the floorboard. "Undo, unbind the magic I find. Set us free. So mote it be."

Ember slammed on the gas again, and our tires screeched on the pavement before lurching us forward once more. We peeled through an intersection as the light turned from yellow to red.

Horns blared behind us, followed by the sounds of metal crunching and glass shattering. I peered through the back window to see the delivery truck on its side in the crossroads and a blue Mazda smashed to bits.

"Please, goddess, don't let anyone die." We'd left enough carnage in our wake as it was.

"Did anyone get a look at the driver? Was it Chrys?" Ember flicked her gaze to the mirror.

"There was a glare on the glass," Miles said. "But I don't think it was her. She's not telekinetic, as far as I know."

"It had to be Boston witches," Shade said. "Either she's working for them or they're working for her."

"And they're trying to keep us away from the church," I said. "She's about to summon Mayhem."

"Then we better stop her." Ember hung a left, finally heading in the direction of our destination, and parked six blocks away. "We'll walk from here. Cloak us, Shade."

"On it." He held his palms toward each other, gathering gray fog between his hands before sending it outward to engulf us, desaturating the world around us.

"Do you want me to cast a silencing spell too?" I asked my sister.

Shade answered, "I can cloak sound too. I was saving my vim, but if you think we need it, I can."

I squelched the laugh that tried to bubble from my chest. He might have apologized, but that ego of his wasn't going anywhere, was it?

"I don't think we need it yet." Ember slid out of the van and closed the door.

The rest of us filed out onto the sidewalk, and we hoofed it across the street, practically running the first three blocks toward the church. When we reached the fourth block, we really ran.

A tourist group stood outside a historical building, taking up most of the sidewalk, and parked cars lined the side of the road, making it nearly impossible to go around them without getting hit by traffic. We slowed to a walk and sidestepped the crowd, but a big, beefy guy decided to take a giant step backward, right into me.

His boot landed on top of my foot, and he lost his balance and careened backward, slamming me onto the hood of a car. I couldn't stop the yelp from escaping my throat or the *oof* as I rolled off the car and smacked the ground.

"What the hell?" He spun around, looking for whatever he smacked into and scratching his head when he found nothing there.

"Ash!" Chaos's deep voice boomed as he rushed toward me, and the entire crowd gasped.

I made a lip-zipping motion and reached for his hand when he offered it. He hauled me up, and I limped as I dragged him away.

"Salem is the most haunted city in America," the tour guide said to his patrons. "Did we just experience an angry ghost?"

With their attention returned to their tour, I stopped half a block away to loosen my laces before my foot swelled. I'd torn a hole in the knee of my fire-proof leggings, but my skin wasn't marred in the slightest.

"Huh. I guess that protection sigil works after all." I wiggled my foot and took a tentative step. The pain was gone. "Nice."

"Almost there," Ember called. "You okay?"

"I'm fine." We caught up with the others and crossed the intersection at a fast clip.

"Shit." Miles stopped in his tracks and grabbed Ember's arm, pulling her back. "I recognize her. She's from BMS."

We peered through our shadow at the woman leaning against a stone fence. She crossed her legs at the ankles and looked down to type on her phone before letting out a sigh and looking right and then left. Her cheeks puffed as she blew out another breath, and she kicked at something on the ground, rubbing the sole of her shoe over the concrete.

"She must be a lookout," Ember said. "How do you know her?"

Miles cringed. "Her name is Wendy. She's the one I convinced to let me into their library. If I'd known she was working with Chrys, I..."

Shade clapped him on the shoulder. "There's a lot we'd all have done differently if we'd known what Chrys was up to."

"I'm sure there are others. We—" I clamped my mouth shut and stepped out of a woman's path, dragging my sister to the edge of the sidewalk. "It's time for a silencing spell if we want to make it in undetected."

She nodded. "Patrice, can you handle that?"

"I—" Shade started, but Ember held up her hand and said, "We're sharing the vim, remember? You're cloaking us. Ash performed sigil magic and the undoing spell in the van. It's someone else's turn."

"Absolutely." Patrice sat in a patch of dead grass next to a fence and mixed a potion. We gathered around her as she recited the incantation, rendering us all soundless to the outside world.

Silent and invisible, we crossed the intersection and headed toward the church. When we reached Wendy, she pressed her phone to her ear. "Hey."

She rolled her eyes, listening to the caller.

"I know. Some High Priestess she'll be. It took her forever to find the damn skull. Then she didn't have the sigil to call on the guy, and once she found that, she had to get another book with summoning instructions. I can't deal with her right now."

We stopped to hear the rest of Wendy's conversation.

"I'm starting to think she's not as big and bad as she made herself out to be." She stuck her finger into her nose and flicked out a booger. Gross.

"Don't you dare report her... Because! We've been on the bottom rung of the ladder for years, and she promised us a seat at the table when she takes over."

"Keep moving." Ember jerked her head toward the church, and we continued up the walk.

"If Chrys wants to take over the coven, why recruit low-level witches?" Miles asked. "She'd have more power with stronger ones."

"The weak ones are easier to control," Chaos said before sucking in a sharp breath.

"What?" I clutched his arm. "What do you feel? Is it Mayhem?"

"Not yet, but she has begun the ceremony. The veil is tearing. We need to hurry." He took off in a jog, so I scurried behind him, making a mental note to seriously work on lengthening my strides.

The others followed, and as we reached the end of the last block, we smashed into an invisible wall of magic. The sensation of claws ripping across my skin made me scream. I pressed my hands to my face, expecting it to be covered in blood, but I didn't have a scratch.

The feeling subsided, and as I looked at my team and then at the church a few yards away, I realized what the ward had done. Our protection sigils had blocked most of the nastiness, but Shade's fog had rolled away, bringing the world into full color. Chrys had stripped us of our cloak, and six dark witches marched toward us.

# CHAPTER 14
# CHAOS

Chrys was a clever witch, setting up her ward far enough away that Ash wouldn't think to begin checking for magic. She'd posted guards outside our home, who had tried to run us off the road as we journeyed here, lookouts a few blocks away, and now more guards to keep us from approaching the building.

She was a clever witch indeed, but she was also a coward, and those souls were the favorites to torture in the Underworld. At least I had something to look forward to when I returned to Hell.

The witches approached from the churchyard, and Ember paced toward them. She did not draw her weapons and instead motioned for us to follow her toward the building. "Let's take this fight off the sidewalk."

"Come on." Ash took my hand. "We can't chance injuring an innocent."

I sent a wave of chaos magic toward our enemies, hoping to scramble their minds and end the confrontation before it began. Nothing happened, which meant Chrys had protected her warriors with whatever spell she'd concocted to block my power.

It didn't matter. Six against six was a fair fight, one I was certain we would win.

A shadow rolled around us, turning everything except our adversaries gray, and I looked at Shade, who shook his head. He didn't cloak us, so one of Chrys's minions had shadow power.

Ember clutched her sword, flames erupting on the blade, and Shade held knives in each hand. Patrice stood next to Ash, both holding potion bottles, and Miles strained, gathering energy between his palms like he had done when Chrys controlled him.

No one made a move.

I glanced at Ash, and she raised her brows, silently asking me to affect their minds. I shook my head, letting her know I'd tried.

Gathering fire in my hands, I eyed the six in front of us. These witches were not innocent, nor were they members of Ash's coven. My promise to cause no harm didn't apply, so I hurled hellfire at the woman closest to me.

She lifted her hand, drawing on the wind and

extinguishing my flames before they reached her. An air witch. Interesting.

"Whatever Chrys has promised you, she's lying." Ash took a step toward them, clutching a potion bottle in each hand. "She's using you, and then she'll discard you when she gets what she wants."

The air witch scoffed. "This is coming from a light witch who summoned a demon." She raised her arms and motioned toward Ash, sending a gust of wind that, if she had been more powerful, would have knocked her off her feet. Instead, it merely blew her hair back.

"Standing tall or on your knees, in the name of the goddess, I force you to freeze." Ash hurled the powdered potion at them. The air witch squealed like a child afraid of a bug and swung her arm, her wind magic just strong enough to blow the spell away before it reached them.

"We don't have time for this." Ember marched toward a man with light hair and swung her extinguished sword, hitting the backs of his legs with the flat side and knocking him to the ground. With a knee on his chest, she pressed the tip of her blade to his throat. "I don't want to kill you, so don't make me."

Another man yelled and tackled Ember, freeing his friend, and chaos ensued.

For once, I wasn't the cause.

Our attempt to enter the church turned into a

magical brawl. Miles threw his energy ball at a brunette. She tried to swat it away with her sword, but his power knocked her off her feet. She careened backward, landing on the ground with a thud, and a redhead screamed and barreled toward him.

I tossed a fireball at her, but her clothing absorbed the flames. Of course Chrys protected her flock against our greatest weapons. If I couldn't use hellfire or mind magic against our foes, I would have to fight like a mundane.

The redhead tackled Miles. I clutched the back of her neck and yanked her off him, letting her dangle in the air while he hit her with a binding spell. When she stopped flailing, I dropped her, and she crumpled onto the ground in a heap.

Ember wrestled with the man on top of her, rolling him to his back and landing a punch to the center of his face. "You're not supposed to kill people," she shouted at me before Patrice poured an orange liquid onto the man, rendering him unconscious.

"No one is dead yet," I replied, though I couldn't make any guarantees about the three remaining witches.

The air witch summoned wind again, blasting it at Ash and, this time, making her stumble. Ash fought back, running toward her and throwing another vial of orange liquid at her face. Again, she blocked the attack with a gust of wind.

I threw another ball of hellfire at her. She waved a hand, attempting to extinguish it, but her magic faltered. Her clothing absorbed most of the blaze. Her hair did not fare so well. Blonde locks went up in flames, and she screamed, calling on her wind to extinguish them. Her magic only made it worse.

"Call your fire back." Ash ran toward me and clutched my arm. "You're going to kill her."

"She is trying to kill us."

"Chaos!" She slapped my shoulder, and I sighed. Sometimes Ash took away all my fun.

"At least put a binding spell on her first." I called back most of the flames, leaving behind a small amount, which she could easily extinguish if she stopped running in circles.

"Patrice is mixing more. We're out."

"You don't need a potion. Simply say the incantation."

She nodded and held a hand toward the burning woman. "Standing tall or on your knees, in the name of the goddess, I force you to freeze."

The woman stopped instantly, a look of sheer agony contorting her features as the small fire reached her scalp. If it were up to me, I would let her burn. Ash, on the other hand, wanted the woman alive, so I called back the fire, ending her suffering.

"Holy crap. It worked." Ash shook her head in disbelief.

Patrice poured the orange liquid onto the air witch's head and lowered her to the ground to sleep. "She needs healing."

"Not our problem." Ember swung her sword at a man. He blocked it with his own blade, the sound of metal hitting metal resonating in my jaw, making it ache.

With Ember taking care of him, only one adversary remained. The shadow witch standing off to the side, straining to keep the scene cloaked. Miles gathered another ball of energy between his palms and hurled it at the man. It hit his chest, and he gasped, his cloak rolling back into him, exposing us all.

"Shade!" Ash shouted as she kneeled by Patrice, helping her mix a spell.

"On it." He gathered his shadow magic and sent it outward, hiding us from view once again.

Patrice poured her sleeping potion on the shadow witch while Ember knocked the other man to the ground. She pinned his shoulders, and Patrice covered his head with the potion as well, neutralizing our final adversary in this battle.

But the war had only just begun.

A low vibration rolled outward from the church, making the fine hairs of my arms stand on end. The energy around us shifted, the thickness indicating Chrys's summoning had nearly reached its apex.

"We must go." I stormed toward the church

entrance, but before I reached the door, my brother's energy registered in my body and I froze. "Ash?"

She slung her restocked bag over her shoulder and rushed toward me. "What's wrong?"

"I sense Mayhem, but she has tricked me before. Is he here?"

She inhaled deeply and closed her eyes. "I think so, yes. Wait, maybe not."

I opened my senses to his vibration, expecting it to wash over me. Instead, it ceased. "Did she summon him only to vanquish him again?"

"I don't know." She snapped her head to the right. "Uh oh."

I followed her gaze to find a massive rift two yards away, where a swarm of fae poured through.

# CHAPTER 15

# ASH

Hecate on a highwire. We did not have time to deal with the friggin' fae. Hundreds of the little buggers flowed through what had to be the biggest rift to date. I couldn't see the actual opening, but the sheer thickness of the swarm indicated a massive tear in the veil.

"I don't suppose you can control these guys like you did the imps?" I started toward the fray, but Chaos clutched my hand.

"I cannot. Ash, try again. Do you sense Mayhem?"

"We need to help the others." I attempted to tug from his grasp, but he tightened his grip.

"With a rift that big, she must have summoned him. I felt him for a moment. I know I did, and if he's in there, we must stop her. She'll use him to raze the entire town."

"I don't know." I looked from our team to him. "It's muffled. She's still cloaking."

"Go," Shade shouted as Miles hit a group of fae with a binding spell. "We'll take care of this."

"Ember?" I started for the door with Chaos.

"I'll be right behind you." She swung her sword, slicing two fae in half with one blow. "Remember, sis, you're at full power now."

Chaos tugged me through the door before I could remind her how much vim I'd already used throwing wasted spells at Chrys's second line of defense. I wasn't at full power. Honestly, the needle on my vim tank struggled to point to the halfway mark.

The sanctuary stood silent. A line of candles, half of them lit, sat on a shelf to the right, and rows of pews led to an ornate altar of carved wood with gold inlays.

We stopped halfway in, and Chaos took both my hands. "Where is he?"

Adrenaline battled with fatigue for control of my psyche. "You're lucky inborn powers like this don't deplete our vim."

"Focus." He squeezed my hands, and I half-expected him to send a pulse of magic through his mark. He stayed true to his promise and let me calm down on my own.

I closed my eyes on a deep inhale and searched for

demonic vibrations. All I felt was the man in front of me, so I switched my focus to Chrys. "Her cloak is still in place, but I'm sure they're in the basement. She'll be as close to the earth as she can get inside a building."

"Which way?"

The tug in my body immediately showed me the path. I pointed to the door to the right of the altar. "Through there. The stairs lead downward."

He nodded and turned, stalking toward the doorway like the predator he was. I followed behind, scanning the chapel for signs of another attack. If anyone lurked in the shadows, waiting for an ambush, they'd hidden themselves well. Did Chrys find another shadow witch to lure to the darker-than-dark side? It wouldn't have surprised me.

I spun in a circle, but no one jumped out, nor did Ember make it inside. Chaos reached the door in three more strides and grabbed the knob. I didn't even have time to shout, "Wait," before he shoved it open with his shoulder.

A massive blast of magic exploded from the door, knocking us both off our feet. I flew backward into a pew, smacking my back against the edge of the wood and tumbling to the floor. My head hit the ground with a *thwack*, and my vision swam, threatening to tunnel into darkness.

I could not let myself pass out. Clutching the sore spot on my scalp, I sat upright and shook my head. The pain faded in a matter of seconds, along with the protection sigil on my arm. Damn. Now that I knew I could make them work, I'd have to come up with a longer-lasting design.

Chaos groaned, and I scrambled to my feet to find him prone on the floor beneath a pew. Blood trickled from his forehead, and I reached to wipe it off before it got into his eye.

"Don't touch that." He knocked my hand away and lifted himself up, hitting his head on the under-side of the bench. "Shit!"

He wiggled out from under the pew before sitting upright. "Demon blood can drive people insane."

I arched a brow. "And you're just now telling me this?"

"Come on." He stood and started for the open door.

"Chaos stop." I grabbed his hand. "Did you learn nothing from that explosion? Let me check for magic first."

He blew out a hard breath. "I can withstand—"

"I can't." I held up my arm and pointed to the empty space the sigil once occupied. "I'm out of protection. Whatever she hits us with, I will feel to my bones...and where is Ember?"

The floor rumbled beneath our feet, the vibration

knocking an ornate cross off the altar. A painting of the Virgin Mary fell from the wall and landed face-down on the floor.

"We don't have time to wait for her." He gestured to the doorway.

I recited the magic-revealing spell, sending sparkles through the entry. A few clung loosely to the remnants of the ward Chaos had set off, but the rest dissipated. "Surely that wasn't her last line of defense."

"She probably didn't expect us to make it this far." He stepped into the hallway and descended the steps.

A crypt lay beneath the church, with four ornate caskets lining the left side. To the right, six more graves had been carved into the wall and covered with granite slabs. The air grew damp the deeper in we ventured, the room narrowing into another hallway before making a sharp right turn.

Chaos stopped at the corner. "Do you need to check for magic?"

"I do, thank you." Though every spell I cast taxed my vim more and more, I recited the incantation. Nothing clung to the walls or floor, so we continued on our way.

The modern concrete floor gave way to worn wood as we approached another staircase. We followed it down into yet another corridor, and before we turned left, Chaos took my hand. "You can use my energy to cast your spell again."

"Actually..." I scrunched my nose as a thought formed in my mind. "I shouldn't need to use a spell. If I can sense people and objects, why not wards and hexes? I found the brooch in the antique shop by searching for magic, so why not?"

The ground rumbled again, and dirt rained from the cracks in the ceiling. Chaos gasped. "I sense him again. Do it quickly before she recharges her cloak."

I centered myself, breathing deeply and searching the basement for signs of magic. The low vibration of a demon other than mine registered in my psyche first. He stood in a room just around the corner. Sending out my feelers, I opened myself to dark magic, waiting for the tell-tale pull.

Everything I felt lay in the room around the corner and down the hall. "Unless her cloak is hiding a ward, I think we're clear."

He looked around the corner, his posture indi-cating he wanted to run. "Do you trust yourself, or do you want to try your spell to be sure?"

I started to consider his words, but the pull was unmistakable. "I'm sure. Mayhem is down there, and there's nothing magical to block our way."

"Very good." He turned the corner, tugging me along.

We crept down this part of the hallway, even the

Prince of Hell showing caution now. My palms slicked with sweat, and I wiped them on my pants. If my heart beat any harder, it might bust through my chest, so I took a deep breath to calm myself.

"What's the plan?" I whispered.

"I will deal with Mayhem. You can handle Chrys."

I laughed. "Can I?"

He stopped abruptly and turned to face me. "Do not doubt yourself, little witch."

"I haven't had time to practice my fire powers."

"You don't need to practice for this. Burn her alive if you have to. Take down the whole church if you must. You know how to call your fire back when you're through, and that is all you need to know." He pinned me with his gaze, the sincerity in his eyes giving me more confidence than I'd ever had before.

"You're right. If there was ever a time for me to start trusting myself, it would be right now." I nodded hard. "I'm ready."

"As am I." His brow slammed down over his eyes, and he flinched. "I no longer feel him. What is Chrys doing?"

"There's only one way to find out." I pointed at the last corner separating us from our final boss battle.

He straightened, curling his hands into fists, and strode into the hallway. The wooden floor ended abruptly, turning into dirt...because of course it did. It wouldn't be the final boss battle if the boss didn't have access to the source of her power.

The hall opened into a massive room with storage shelves lining the walls and a summoning circle taking up the center of the floor. Black candles, still burning, sat at each of the pentagram's five points, and... Was that Mayhem's skull resting in the center?

Chaos cocked his head and squinted at the skull. "What in Hell's name?"

"It's about damn time you got here." Chrys stepped out of the shadows, her eyes wild, her dark hair disheveled. She stopped by the circle, narrowing her eyes to glare at me. "Who helped you escape?"

My fire magic rose to simmer just below the surface, and I forced a neutral expression. "Does it matter?"

"I suppose not. Shame on me for acting like a Bond villain and running away without watching you die. I won't make that mistake twice."

Chaos couldn't tear his gaze away from his brother's skull. "What are you doing with Mayhem? Have you not summoned him?"

She strolled closer to us. "Oh, I've summoned him."

I took two steps back. "Did you vanquish him again?"

"Shut up. I know who he is." She clutched her head. "Yes, I know what he's capable of."

I glanced at Chaos, and his eyes widened in realization at the same time as mine. Did Chrys just do what I thought she did? Surely she was smarter than that.

"I said shut up! I don't care what you are!" She flung her arms to her sides and raised them, causing the ground to rumble and crack.

I grabbed Chaos's arm and tugged him toward the door, but the earth split between us, a fissure widening, separating us until I couldn't reach him. Chrys might not have been smart enough to summon a demon correctly, but she was still as powerful as all get out.

The building creaked above us, straining against the shift in the foundation. If we didn't stop her now, she'd bury us all beneath its weight.

Chaos threw hellfire at her. She waved her hand, and a thick root spiraled up, absorbing the flames. She stepped around it, patting the uncharred surface. "Do you know how much vim it takes to fireproof these? The sooner I get rid of you the better."

She pointed, and another root shot from the ground to snake toward Chaos. He stomped it before it could ensnare his leg and reached down to grab it, yanking it so hard, it snapped and shriveled away.

Jerking her head toward me, she sent out another root. Before it could grip my ankle, I darted right, yanked a dagger from my thigh holster, and stabbed the sucker, pinning it to the dirt. Yay for speed sigils.

Chrys clutched her head again, reminding me of the pounding headache Chaos had given me when he'd roared inside my mind. I'd learn my lesson about saying spells loud enough for her to hear them, so I called on what little vim I had left and whispered the binding spell.

"Standing tall or on your knees, by the—"

"Aarrgh!" Ember charged in with her sword ablaze, screaming like a banshee. She swung it like a baseball bat, hitting Chrys with the flat side, right in her stomach. My sister spun, this time aiming for her back, but with speed faster than any sigil could provide, Chrys turned and grabbed the flaming blade with both hands before yanking it out of her grasp.

Ember's sword was razor-sharp. It should have sliced right through Chrys's palms, but when she tossed it aside, her hands appeared unscathed.

Chaos hurled another fireball. This one hit her in the chest. Her fireproof shirt deflected it, and she rolled her neck before flashing a sinister smile. "Brother."

My demon's nostrils flared on his exhale. "Mayhem."

"Holy Hades." I cut my gaze between them. "It took you days to break through and take over my body, and he did it in a few minutes."

"That's because I was holding back." Chaos made a face at me, letting me know I wasn't helping, before scaling Chrys's fissure to stand in front of me.

"Why are you helping these witches?" Her eyes widened and narrowed like Chrys was fighting to take control away from Mayhem. "Kill them."

Chaos crossed his arms. "No. I must reason with you, brother."

Ember charged toward her, daggers drawn, but with Mayhem in control, she...they...dodged the attack, stepping aside and using my sister's momentum to throw her into a shelving unit. Books, bowls, and artifacts tumbled down with the impact, and a cast-iron pot smacked her on the head. Ember grunted and keeled over, her lids barely fluttering.

"Em!" I started toward her.

Chrys/Mayhem spun toward me, and a garbled yell ripped from her throat. "Not that one! I need her alive." She'd clawed her way back to the surface.

"Standing tall—"

"No, Ash." She flicked her wrist, and dozens upon dozens of roots rose from the ground.

My speed sigil hadn't run out of juice, so I shot across the room as fast as The Flash. Sadly, the roots were faster. A thin one struck like a viper, slashing through my fireproof pants before encircling my ankle. I tumbled, smacking my shoulder on the dirt and grunting as a mess of the sorry suckers ensnared me, rolling me to my back and strapping me to the ground. Again.

I started to whisper the freezing spell, but she sent another root across my face, gagging me like she'd done before. I bit down, determined to chew through it, bitterness flooding my tongue.

And the rest of the dozens of roots penetrating the dirt? She'd trapped Chaos and built a cage over my unconscious sister in thirty seconds flat. I hoped to Hecate the rest of our team had dealt with the fae and were on their way.

Chrys clutched her head, her face pinching in agony. Chaos morphed into his demon form, and, with a guttural roar, he set his entire body ablaze. Heat from his hellfire blasted my cheeks, and I struggled against the roots, which only made them tighter.

He extinguished his flames, and the roots remained unscathed. Roaring again, he flexed, straining against his prison. It stretched with him, tightening again when he relaxed. "Mayhem, release me."

"I'm in control." Chrys shuffled toward me with an unsteady gait. Dark circles ringed her eyes, and she heaved in a breath. "If you can get this demon out of me, I promise to kill you quickly."

"Why ith he in oo?" I mumbled around my gag. "Oo had hith kull."

Chaos continued straining against his binding. Ember didn't move. I could imagine how depleted Chrys must've been. No doubt she used most of her vim on fire- and demon-proofing the roots holding him.

"I'm going to remove your gag, but so help me Hecate, if you try that damn freezing spell again, I will send the root through one cheek and out the other, taking half of your teeth with it."

Well, that sounded painful. I nodded my agreement, and the gag snaked away to rest two inches from my face, the sharp end pointed directly at me. "Why is he inside you?"

She shoved up her sleeve, showing me Mayhem's mark on her arm. "I wanted to control him like you control Chaos, so I did this."

How long had Chrys been learning sigil magic? "I don't control him. He helps me because he loves me."

"Lies." She tapped a finger to her temple. "He says that's not possible. Chaos would never be stupid enough to fall for a witch."

"It's true, brother." Chaos stopped straining. "Ash is mine. She has claimed me, so you will not harm her."

"Please, Chrys," I said. "You've got to perform an exorcism or Mayhem will burn through your body and use your very essence to reform."

"Shut up! Let me think." She jabbed her fingers

into her hair and pulled before whirling toward me. "Do it. Exorcise him. He's driving me crazy."

Chaos scoffed. "What did you think would happen when you invited a Prince of Hell called Mayhem into your mind?"

"You shut up too." She flicked her wrist, tightening the roots around him. "Help me get him out of my head, and I'll let you live."

"I can't." And even if I could, I didn't buy her lies for a single hot second.

"Yes, you can. You did it with that one." She jerked her thumb toward Chaos, who had resumed straining against the roots.

I couldn't imagine how much vim she put into creating them if he still couldn't bust through like he'd done at Shade's house. Yet she stayed on her feet, thanks to Mayhem no doubt.

She flicked her wrist at me, and the roots pulled away from the ground, jerking me upright. The pointy end of one pressed against my cheek, ready to rip my mouth apart if I tried to cast a spell.

It was time to take stock and figure out a plan. Most likely, she didn't fireproof my prison. I could burn through it right now and go after her, but with Chaos restrained and my sister out of commission, it would be me against Super Chrys, and there was no way I could defeat her/Mayhem on my own.

Sometimes knowing your limitations was a good thing.

"Do you have a grimoire with exorcisms?" I asked, trying to keep a good poker face. "I can help you, but I need a book. I don't speak Latin, nor do I know the spell by heart."

She narrowed her eyes and backed toward the table, her gaze never straying from me. "Don't try anything."

"How could I?"

Chrys finally tore her gaze away from me to look at the grimoire in front of her. She flipped through the pages, muttering, "Shut up, shut up, shut up," as she searched for the spell. I could only imagine the things Mayhem was saying in her mind.

She turned the pages forward and back again, frustration making her movements jerky. "This is all about using demons to do your bidding. I don't see anything about exorcising them."

"Try the index." If I could convince her to free me, I wouldn't have to reveal my unlocked power. Then maybe I could exorcise Mayhem and lock him in a containment circle. With Chrys's depleted vim, I could defeat her easily if she didn't have a Prince of Hell coming in and out of control. Then Chaos could deal with his brother.

She flipped to the back of the book and ran her

finger down the pages. "Nothing. There's nothing. If you can't help me, I might as well kill you now."

Ember groaned and pushed onto her elbow. Chaos had gone utterly still as if he were meditating, but at Chrys's words, his eyes flew open. She slammed the book shut and marched toward me as Shade, Miles, and Patrice darted into the room.

# CHAPTER 16

# ASH

"It's about damn time." I called on my magic, curling my fingers toward my palms and igniting fireballs in each hand. The flames licked up my arms and danced across my chest and down my legs, incinerating the roots holding me captive.

Chrys faltered, her eyes widening and her mouth falling open, which gave the others just enough time to start their attack.

"Holy shit, Ash," Shade said as he threw a dagger. Chrys dodged it easily, and it stuck into the dirt three feet from Ember's cage.

My sister reached through the roots, her fingers grazing the knife, but she couldn't grab it. Chaos strained again, roaring and setting his demonic form ablaze. The roots holding him groaned against his strength, a thin one splitting, hanging on only by a few fibers.

"Are these friends of yours too, brother?" Chrys smiled menacingly. "I will enjoy cracking their necks one by one."

"You will not harm them." He strained again, and the roots thinned even more.

Miles threw an energy ball, knocking her shoulder back. She snapped her gaze to him, and Patrice uncorked a potion. She managed two words of the spell when Chrys bent her fingers into claws. The ground rumbled, another fissure opening beneath our healer.

I lunged for Ember's discarded sword, grabbing it by the hilt and rolling twice. Patrice screamed, her speed sigil obviously depleted, and fell into the hole. Shade dove for her, reaching for her hand. Their fingers barely brushed before she disappeared entirely.

Scrambling to my feet, I hacked at my sister's cage. Her sword slashed through the enclosure, making a hole just big enough for her to wiggle through. "She's got Mayhem inside her," I said, and I grabbed Miles's dagger from the dirt. "Help me free Chaos."

We darted toward him, but with one final, guttural roar, he tore through his prison and stormed toward Chrys. He took three steps when a root jutted from the ground and pierced his chest. He stumbled and fell to his knees.

"No!" I screamed and rushed to my demon, clutching his shoulders, the rest of the fray fading into the background. Tears streamed down my cheeks, my stomach clenching, wrenching my heart down into it. I wasn't ready to let him go. "Please tell me you have multiple hearts that have to be pierced before you're vanquished."

Chaos groaned and pulled the root from his chest. "I have one, and he barely nicked it. That was a warning..." He snapped his head toward Chrys. "Which I will not heed."

"Have it your way," she said, and the ground exploded beneath Miles and Shade, sending them flying toward the outer wall. The moment their backs made impact, vines jutted out, wrapping around them and pinning them, their feet dangling four feet from the ground.

Ember rushed toward them, leaping over the fissure that had consumed Patrice. She hacked at the biggest root, splitting it apart. Three more grew in its place. "Damn hydras."

"This must stop, Mayhem." Chaos rose to his feet and stepped in front of me. "These witches are not the enemy."

"All witches are the enemy, and as soon as I'm finished enjoying this one's power, I will burn through her and kill her too." Chrys's eyes widened in alarm. She must've been scrambling to gain control, and for once, I wished she'd succeed.

"Standing tall or on your knees, in the name of the goddess, I force you to freeze!" I sent my magic out to Chrys, but effing Mayhem still had control. She flicked her wrist, and a wall of rocks jutted from the ground, stopping my spell in its tracks.

Ember pulled at the binds holding Shade and Miles, her hands engulfed in flames. Chrys snapped her fingers, and they tightened, squeezing the guys until they wheezed. I had no idea if Patrice was alive, but the way Shade's eyeballs bulged from their sockets said he wouldn't be much longer.

"Let them go!" Panic laced Ember's scream, turning it feral as she hacked and pulled, burned, and clawed at the roots killing our friends.

"Brother, stop." Chaos marched around the rock wall, his taloned fingers curled into fists, and I rushed to keep up.

"I warned you," Chrys said, and another root shot toward my demon's heart.

I swung the dagger with all my might, slicing through it before it reached its destination. Chaos knocked it aside and stood face-to-face with Chrys/Mayhem. I glanced at my arm. The speed and strength sigils faded away, leaving plain old *just* Ash behind.

And *just* Ash was all I needed. She always had been.

"Chrys, I know you're in there." I stepped in front of Chaos. "I can see it in your eyes. You have to find a way back to the surface. Take back control, and we can help you."

A sinister laugh erupted from her chest. "No witch can defeat Mayhem, Prince of Hell, destroyer —."

"Of armies and all who vex him. Yeah, I've heard that line before, and I'm not buying it." I crossed my arms. "Seems like the entire reason you're here is because a witch defeated you."

She growled and sent a root spiraling up my leg. I grabbed it with a burning hand, turning it to soot.

"Focus on your earth magic, Chrys. Cling to it, and let it propel you to the top. I had to do the same thing when Chaos took control of me."

Her eyes blinking rapidly, she let out a garbled groan. "This body...no longer belongs to the witch."

The ground trembled. The walls shook. The earth opened beneath my sister's feet. She clung to the vines that trapped Shade with one hand, swinging as the bottom dropped out from under her.

My head spun and my insides quivered as my heart took off in a sprint. "Come on, Chrys. You can do it. Take control."

"Give it to her, Mayhem," Chaos ordered, though I

doubted his brother enjoyed being told what to do any more than he did.

"I won't." She clutched her head, her face scrunching in agony. Dragging her fingers down her cheeks, she thrashed from side to side. "This body is... This body is..."

I glanced at my sister. Her grip on the vine slipped, and she nearly let go.

"Drop your sword, Em," I shouted.

She held on by three fingers. Shade and Miles hung limp, their skin turning blue. Ember looked at her sword, her baby, and I swore to Hecate if she fell into oblivion because she refused to let it go, I would never forgive her.

"Aaahhh! This body is mine!" Chrys gasped, her eyes flying wide as she panted. "Shut up!" She spun and flailed, colliding with a shelf and sending a mess of two-by-fours clattering to the ground.

Ember huffed and released her sword, letting it fall into the abyss as she used both hands to drag herself up and get a foothold in the vines.

Chrys clutched the shelf, heaving breaths, fighting to maintain control. I searched in the core of my being for any vim I might have left and cast one last spell. "Standing tall or on your knees..." Ember joined me for the rest. "In the name of the goddess, we force you to freeze."

Our magic shot out, and, with Chrys finally in

control, she wasn't fast enough to block it. She stilled, the look of panic in her eyes palpable. I remembered that feeling too well.

"How long will she remain bound?" Chaos placed his hand on my lower back, and I nearly jumped out of my skin. "Not long enough. Can you free them?" I shouted at my sister.

The roots and vines Chrys had summoned continued to squeeze the life out of the guys, as she had said would happen to me in New Orleans. Ember hauled a leg up to remove a knife from her boot, and she sawed through the one closest to Shade's throat. When it didn't multiply, she cut the one around his chest.

"One problem." She freed his arm. "There's no ground beneath us."

The crevice stretched seven feet wide and who knew how deep. She might have been able to crawl across the vines to the edge and make her escape, but the unconscious Miles and Shade wouldn't stand a chance.

"Can you reach Miles? Cut him some slack so he can breathe."

"I think so."

"What is your plan?" Chaos asked.

"First, we have to cast a containment ring around her in case Mayhem busts through the bind. Then, we're going to build a bridge."

My satchel lay abandoned a few yards away, so I grabbed it and pulled out my shaker of salt. Chrys's demonic grimoire held the incantation needed to trap a demon, and I opened right to the page. I pulled her away from the wall and poured a ring around her before scanning the words.

"Do you have enough vim for this?" Chaos asked.

"Sure don't. That's why I said *we* have to cast the circle." I slipped my hand into his.

"Demon magic can't be used to create a demon trap. My very nature will fight against it."

"And my very nature will counter yours. Have you forgotten we were meant to be together?"

"I could never forget. We are halves of the same whole." He squeezed my hand, sending a pulse of power into me.

My body electrified, my nerves hummed back to life with a blast of adrenaline that would keep a normal witch awake for days. I scanned the book one more time to be sure I had the words right, and I recited the Latin. Chaos's nature did try to fight back, but only for a moment. I channeled it into my being, turning it on its head and activating the circle like it was the easiest thing in the world. Honestly, it kind of was.

We broke contact, and I expected a wave of fatigue to crash into me like it had done in the past. But I felt fine when Chaos took back his magic. Even a bit energized. The bond I had with my demon kept growing and doing amazing things.

"Shade's not breathing," Ember shouted from across the room, spurring me into action.

"Grab those slats of wood." I pointed, and Chaos, still in demon form, scooped up twenty of them like they were toothpicks and carried them to the offending fissure.

Boy, oh boy, was that thing deep. I could see the bottom at least, but it must've gone twenty feet down. The guys would break their necks if we cut them free and let them fall.

"Patrice?" I yelled. "Are you still with us?"

"I'm here," her voice sounded tiny, but she was able to respond. Whew.

"How will you build a bridge with no nails or fasteners?" he asked.

"With physics." I began lining up the beams four across. I placed a perpendicular slat and then lay four more on top of it. Another perpendicular piece went across the center of those, and then four more. When I finished, I had an arched bridge that could easily stretch across the fissure...on one condition. "How far can you jump?"

Chaos chuckled and moved to one end of the bridge. We lifted it in unison, and I rushed forward as he leaped across with the grace of a panther. With the bridge in place, he tested its sturdiness. "You're quite clever."

"It happens when you read a lot."

He stood in the center of my creation, and Ember cut the rest of the vines holding Miles, dropping him into my demon's arms. He lay him on his back in the dirt before returning to the bridge to help down Shade.

My former nemesis's lips had gone white, the skin on his face pale blue. I checked for a pulse, but if he had one, it was too weak to detect. Tipping his head back, I pinched his nose and blew two deep breaths into his mouth. His chest rose and fell with my effort, but he didn't move.

"Come on. You can't make amends and then die on me." I clasped my hands over his chest and pumped his heart. When nothing happened, I gave him a few more breaths. Still nothing, so I pumped again. I breathed again, repeating the cycle three more times.

Miles moaned and rolled to his side. Ember found a rope in the mess Chrys had made of the space, and she and Chaos worked on retrieving Patrice.

Still, Shade didn't move. I checked for a pulse and again found nothing. My hand beneath his nose didn't pick up the slightest breath. "Listen to me, you goober. This can't be your final eff you. Wake. The. Hell. Up." I pumped his chest with each word and blew the biggest breath I could into his mouth.

He coughed. Then he sputtered and rolled to his side, gasping for air. A coughing fit racked his body, making him curl into the fetal position as he hacked and gasped, hacked and gasped.

I sat back on my butt in the dirt, my head spinning. When he could breathe normally again, he tried to sit up. I helped him get upright and rubbed his back.

"When I said I wasn't over you yet, I never dreamed it would make you kiss me." He smirked and laughed, which turned into another cough.

"Dream on." I slapped his shoulder and laughed before rising to my feet and dusting the dirt off my pants. "You okay, Miles?"

He took a deep breath and rubbed his chest. "I've been better, but I'll survive."

"We all will," Ember said, and I turned around to find Patrice sitting next to her on the ground.

I allowed myself to feel three seconds of relief before I gestured to Chrys. "She won't if we don't do something fast."

# CHAPTER 17

# ASH

"If your circle is as strong as the ones she cast, you can leave her be and let Mayhem take over her form." Chaos crossed his arms, eyeing the still-frozen Chrys in the circle. "She deserves worse."

"Nobody deserves to go through that, believe me." I patted his shoulder.

He jerked away, whirling toward me. "Have you forgotten everything she's done?"

I put my hands on my hips and raised my chin. No, I had not, but I wouldn't wish that on my greatest enemy, who, at the moment, happened to be the witch in question.

"We haven't forgotten." Ember paced around the circle. "Have you forgotten we're light witches? We don't kill people."

"On purpose," I added, which earned me an eye roll from my sister.

"Can you…" She gestured to his demonic junk hanging free since he'd torn through his clothes. "Ash might enjoy the view, but the rest of us do not."

"If I return to my human form, I will still be naked. Would you enjoy that view more?"

"Actually…" I opened my bag and pulled out the extra set of clothes I'd packed for him. "I had a feeling you might go full-demon."

He accepted the clothing, turned on his heel, and stormed away.

"Somebody's got his panties in a wad," Ember muttered.

"She has done some pretty bad things." I shrugged and zipped my bag.

"Whoa, Ash." She held up her hands. "Are you actually suggesting we do nothing and let Mayhem absorb her? Because, if so, we need to freeze you too. I won't let you turn dark."

Now it was my turn for an eye roll. "No, I'm not suggesting that. I just mean I can see where he's coming from. He's protective, and she hurt us all."

"We're performing an exorcism." Ember cocked a brow, challenging me to argue. "We need answers."

I crossed my arms. "Then we have to send someone home because we don't have the supplies to do it here. I didn't count on her possessing herself, or I would have brought the book with me."

Chaos returned to my side, in human form and fully clothed. "Thank you," he whispered, and I smiled.

"Can't we take her with us? It would be faster than a round trip." Patrice handed Shade the healing drink she'd been mixing.

I shook my head. "If we want her to survive, the exorcism has to happen in the place she was possessed."

"I can go get it," Miles said. "How long will the infantry be asleep outside?"

"At least another hour or two," Patrice said. "Are you sure you're up to it? You were unconscious for quite a while."

"I never stopped breathing." Miles clutched Shade's shoulder with brotherly affection, and Ember tossed him the keys. "Where's the book?"

"The cabinet in my studio," I said. "Bring the candles and salt with you too. It's all in there from..."

"Here." Patrice handed him a potion bottle. "Cast a shadow spell, just to be safe."

"Thanks." He turned and strode away.

"Are they all still lying in the churchyard?" I rummaged through my bag again and found two more binding potions.

"We dragged them around back and propped

them against the building." Shade drained his cup and handed it back to Patrice. "Thanks for that."

She wiped it with a magic-neutralizing cloth. "It's what I do."

Ember nodded at the vials. "Are those the freezing potions? I've got enough vim for one more spell. Maybe two, but that would leave you on your own for the exorcism. We need Patrice to save her vim in case healing is required."

Shade lifted his hands in a WTF gesture. "She won't be alone. I'm still here."

Ember cut her gaze between us. "I'm not used to you two playing nicely together. Sure you're up to it?"

He stretched his neck and rolled his shoulders. "Good as new. Patrice is a goddess-send."

Our healer's cheeks flushed pink. "I'm glad I can help, but when this is through, I'd like to go back to the sanctity of my kitchen and stay there."

"Amen, sister." I gave her a high-five.

Chrys's fingers twitched, and Ember dumped a bottle of binding potion on her before reciting the incantation.

"If she's in a containment circle, why do you have to keep her frozen?" Shade asked.

"The spell freezes him inside her too," Chaos said. "It's the only thing that kept me from destroying Ash when our situation was dire."

Shade laughed dryly. "Damn."

"Indeed." My demon rested his hand on my back. "If you break the summoning circle, I will retrieve my brother's skull."

"I'll get it." Ember scooped up the skull and gasped. "I can feel his energy." She used her teeth to pull her sleeves over her hands, breaking the skin-to-skull contact. "He feels different than Chaos."

"He's a different demon," I said. "Do you think the rest of her minions gave up?"

"It sounded like they were already losing faith in her." Ember set the skull on the table and rubbed her palms on her pants. "They probably decided to cut their losses and pretend it never happened. That's what I'd do if I joined a failed coup."

Half an hour and one last binding spell later, Miles returned with my supplies and laid them out on the table.

Shade grabbed a candle and the exorcism book. "You didn't really have a stomach bug that day. This is what you had to clean up, isn't it?"

"Yep." I took the book and opened it to the containment spell. The one I'd cast around Chrys wouldn't be nearly strong enough once we released Mayhem. "Set the candles at the five points of the pentagram. We need to make this one stronger than we've ever done before."

I poured a second ring of salt around Chrys and sent a controlled flame to each candle.

Shade and Patrice looked at me in wonder. "How?" she asked.

I waved off her question. "My magic was bound. I'll tell you about it later."

"And you?" she asked Miles. "The energy balls you can create...that's new."

He lowered his gaze, his shoulders rising toward his ears. "Chrys drew it out of me. She made me swear not to tell anyone until I'd perfected it."

"That tracks." I shook my head. Our former friend was a master manipulator.

Chrys's hands curled and splayed. A moan emanated from her throat.

"She's coming to. Hurry." I grabbed Shade's and Chaos's hands while Ember held the book out for us to read. Chaos sent a rush of demon magic into me, setting my nerves ablaze. I massaged it, softening it before opening up and sending some into Shade.

He gasped, shuddering before straightening his spine, and we read the incantation in unison, activating the stronger circle without a nanosecond to spare.

Chrys jolted upright, her eyes wild as she clutched her head. "You have to help me."

"We're trying to." I grabbed the skull, ready to toss it into the circle, but I paused. "Hold on."

"Release me!" Mayhem shouted through Chrys, scrambling to her feet. Her shoulder slammed against the invisible wall, making the magic shimmer.

"Not a chance." Ember clutched a dagger in each hand. "Put the skull in the circle, sis."

"I don't think I should." I returned it to the table.

Chaos jerked his head toward me, glowering. "If you exorcise him without it, he will not be able to reform. You'll have to vanquish him to his prison in Hell."

"You wouldn't dare," Chrys growled. "Brother, stop them."

Chaos looked at Chrys and then at me, his expression softening. "What is your plan?"

"He's not a happy camper, and whether we exorcise him with his skull or he burns through Chrys, he doesn't owe us a thing because we didn't free him." I drummed my fingers on top of the skull. "We need some kind of leverage."

My demon straightened his spine. "You have me."

"And he's listened to you fabulously so far." Ember sheathed one dagger, clutching the other tightly. "Ash is right. I don't know what Chrys did to keep the mundane away from this church, but they'll be back eventually. If we let him reform here, we'll have to deal with transporting him back to the house."

"Chaos!" Chrys roared before her eyes widened and she clawed at her face. "Do it. Do whatever you have to do. Just get him out of my head."

He gazed into my eyes, and a full five seconds passed before he nodded. "Agreed." He turned to Chrys. "We will call you back, brother. Have patience."

"Patience?" Chrys's voice grew garbled. "What have these witches done to you? Kill them. Kill them and set me free." She slammed her fists against the circle, and the magic pulsed. The dark brown of her irises rippled with purple. Her nails broke the skin, drawing bloody claw marks down her cheeks.

"It's now or never." I grabbed my demon's hand. "Get ready to pull her out, Em."

Patrice rushed to the table to mix a healing potion while Shade held the book in front of me.

"What can I do?" Miles asked.

"How well can you pronounce Latin?" I held my hand toward him, and he took it.

"Don't let them do this! Yes. Yes, they have to!" Chrys alternated with Mayhem, her fists clenched, every muscle in her body straining.

Miles and I read the words.

"No!" she shouted. "I'll make you a deal."

"Don't take it," Chaos said.

"Didn't plan to." I squeezed Miles's hand, and we read the incantation again. On the third refrain, the walls shook. Chrys gasped and doubled over. A deafening pop resounded from somewhere inside her, and the tendons in her neck protruded until I thought they'd rip through her skin.

She stood upright, her mouth agape as she threw her head back and let out a blood-curdling scream. Purple smoke poured from her mouth and nose. She wheezed another breath, and more smoke rushed out with her exhale. Her third breath was clean, so Ember grabbed her arm and yanked her out of the circle.

The smoke billowed inside the ring, spiraling upward before crashing into the wall. The magic pulsed. Then it cracked.

Oh, shit. Crappity crap. "Why is he still here?"

"You must vanquish him," Chaos said matter-of-factly, as if that was a detail I should have already known. "If he breaks free, he will possess another person."

"You could have told me that ahead of time." I grabbed the book from Shade.

"I believe I did." Ever the helpful demon he was.

I took a deep breath and centered myself, willing my pulse and my breathing to slow before I passed out. Focusing my intention on a vanquishing spell, I flipped through the pages. "Here." I shoved the book into Shade's arms and took Chaos's and Miles's hands once more.

We recited the incantation. Nothing happened. Mayhem billowed, gathering his smoke into a ball and straining against the magic wall. Another crack.

We said the words three more times, and still nothing happened.

Chaos peered at the book. "I believe the third word is pronounced with a long E."

"Now you tell me."

Three more cracks formed in the magic. The biggest fissure began to split, a tiny stream of Mayhem smoke seeping through.

We tried the incantation again, hoping to Hecate we pronounced everything right this time. Mayhem continued seeping through the circle. The second recitation didn't help. Smoke spiraled upward, circling above Ember's head. She had no clue what was happening. She and Patrice continued attempting to revive Chrys, oblivious to the danger of our battle.

"Oh, hell no. Not my sister." I squeezed Chaos's hand, and he sent another ginormous pulse of magic into me. I shared it with Miles, and we recited the words a third time, giving it everything we had.

The smoke froze. Then it crackled. The once-billowy essence of Mayhem turned to thin shards of glass. A visible rift tore open inside the circle, sucking his rigid form through, but the part of him outside the wall slammed against the magic, unable to pass.

"Watch out." I raced to the containment ring and dropped to the ground, skidding across it like I was sliding into home base. My boot broke the circle, and the rest of Mayhem disappeared through the rift before it slammed shut, holding him on the other side.

"Holy Hecate." I flopped onto my back and panted. "Is he gone?"

Chaos stood over me. "He is, and he won't be happy when he returns. With any of us."

I waved off his words and dropped my arm on the floor. "That's a problem for tomorrow."

"Wake up," Ember said, and Chrys wheezed.

I rolled to my stomach to find everyone but Chaos kneeling around her. My demon offered his hand, and I let him tug me to my feet before I sagged in his arms. He helped me walk to the team and held me as I peered at our once-powerful adversary. Our once-friend.

Her lids fluttered, her head rolling from side to side. She opened her mouth, and a whisper crossed her lips.

"What did she say?" I wrapped my arms around Chaos, letting his warm, strong embrace envelope me.

"I can't hear her." Ember patted her cheek gently. "Chrys, what are you trying to say?"

"I..." Chrys squeezed her eyes shut as if speaking pained her. "I had...no choice."

Ember sat back on her heels. "Oh you definitely did, and you made the wrong one."

"No." Her voice was breathy, barely audible. "I had to." Her face relaxed, her body going limp.

Miles brought a hand to his lips. "Is she...?"

Patrice pressed two fingers to her neck and then

her wrist. She held her hand beneath Chrys's nose and shook her head. "She's gone."

A collective sigh rushed out of us all, and we stood there, saying nothing, doing nothing, for several minutes. We had neutralized the threat. We had the skull and the sigils, and we could finally move forward with our attempt to lift my curse. I had unlocked my magic and fallen in love. We had won.

So, why did it feel so much like we'd lost?

Chaos cleared his throat, breaking the silence. "We need to leave before the mundane come back. Shall I cremate her?"

"No." I wiped the mist from my eyes. "She was our friend. We'll give the body to her mom."

Ember sniffled. "That's the right thing to do. Gather your stuff, and let's head to the van. Cloak us, Shade."

Chaos cradled Chrys in his arms and carried her as we made our way through the labyrinth of tunnels to the ground floor. Mayhem's skull rested inside my satchel, and no one spoke on the fifteen-minute ride home.

We left her body in the basement—Patrice casting a preservation spell on her remains until her mother could retrieve her—and made our way upstairs. It would take time to process everything we'd won and all we had lost, but the energy in the house already felt lighter.

Ember opened the fridge and handed a beer to each of us. "To bittersweet endings. May Chrys finally find peace." We clinked our bottles in a toast, and I took a long pull from mine. The effervescent bubbles cooled me on their way down, reminding me that we were still very much alive, and our quest had barely begun.

"She said she had no choice." I laced my fingers with Chaos's. "What do you think she meant?"

"Rantings of a madwoman." Shade took a drink. "Mayhem nearly had her; I'm sure he scrambled her brain."

"Indeed," Chaos said. "He was moments away from overcoming her. Even if she had survived, she would not have been herself. I'm surprised she spoke at all."

"What do we do now?" Patrice asked.

"Now we rest," Ember said. "Recharge, recover, live to fight another day."

"I'll drink to that." Miles clinked his bottle to hers.

We finished our beer, and everyone headed to their respective bedrooms. I set my satchel on the dresser, but Chaos opened a drawer and slipped it inside.

"Don't want him watching us sleep?" I rose onto my toes and pressed a kiss to his lips.

"Not really." He slid his arms around me, holding

me tightly. "I'd rather have one last night alone with my little witch."

I leaned back to look into his eyes. "This won't be our last night. We'll figure something out."

"We will try our best." He kissed my forehead, lingering there as he inhaled. "Right now…"

"Is all that matters." I angled my head up to brush his lips with mine.

He smiled, though it didn't reach his eyes. "I can't promise you the *happy ever after* you deserve."

I rested my hands on his shoulders, looking at him with all the sincerity I felt in every fiber of my being. "I'll settle for *happy for now*."

He shook his head. "It's so much more than now. I will be by your side until the bitter end."

"Okay." I cupped his cheek in my hand, and he nuzzled into it. "How about *happy until the inevitable?*"

The corners of his eyes crinkled as he curved his lips. "*Happy until the inevitable*. That, I can promise."

**The saga continues in Mayhem and Ember…**

# Also by Carrie Pulkinen

**New Orleans Nocturnes Series**

License to Bite

Shift Happens

Life's a Witch

Santa Got Run Over by a Vampire

Finders Reapers

Swipe Right to Bite

Batshift Crazy

Collection One: Books 1-3

Collection Two: Books 4 - 7

**Crescent City Wolf Pack Series**

Werewolves Only

Beneath a Blue Moon

Bound by Blood

A Deal with Death

A Song to Remember

Shifting Fate

Collection One: Books 1-3

Collection Two: Books 4-6

**Haunted Ever After Series**

Love at First Haunt

Second Chance Spirit

Third Time's a Ghost

Love and Ghosts

Love and Omens

Love and Curses

Collection One: Books 1 - 3

Collection Two: Books 4 - 6

**Fire Witches of Salem Series**

Chaos and Ash

Commanding Chaos

Claiming Chaos

**Stand Alone Books**

Flipping the Bird

Sign Steal Deliver

Azrael

Lilith

The Rest of Forever

Soul Catchers

Bewitching the Vampire

# ABOUT THE AUTHOR

Carrie Pulkinen is a paranormal romance author who has always been fascinated with things that go bump in the night. Of course, when you grow up next door to a cemetery, the dead (and the undead) are hard to ignore. Pair that with her passion for writing and her love of a good happily-ever-after, and becoming a paranormal romance author seems like the only logical career choice.

Before she decided to turn her love of the written word into a career, Carrie spent the first part of her professional life as a high school journalism and yearbook teacher. She loves good chocolate and bad puns, and in her free time, she likes to read, drink wine, and travel with her family.

*Connect with Carrie online:*
www.CarriePulkinen.com